M000073537

DESTROYED
WITH YOU
J. KENNER

NEW YORK TIMES BESTSELLING AUTHOR

Also By The Author

STARK SECURITY
shattered with you
shadows of you-short story
broken with you
ruined with you
wrecked with you

THE STARK SAGA
novels
release me
claim me
complete me
anchor me
lost with me
novellas
take me
have me
play my game
seduce me
unwrap me
deepest kiss
entice me
hold me
please me
indulge me
cherish me

Praise for J. Kenner's Novels

"*Shattered With You* is a sultry little page turner that comes brimming with scorching passion, edge of your seat action, and heart-wrenching emotion." *Reds Romance Reviews*

"J. Kenner is an exceptional storyteller. The drama, tension, and heat were perfect." *About That Story*

"PERFECT for fans of *Fifty Shades of Grey* and *Bared to You*. *Release Me* is a powerful and erotic romance novel." *Reading, Eating & Dreaming Blog*

"I will admit, I am in the 'I loved *Fifty Shades*' camp, but after reading *Release Me*, Mr. Grey only scratches the surface compared to Damien Stark." *Cocktails and Books Blog*

"It is not often when a book is so amazingly well-written that I find it hard to even begin to accurately describe it . . . " *Romancebookworm's Reviews*

DESTROYED
WITH **YOU**
J. KENNER

NEW YORK TIMES BESTSELLING AUTHOR

M&O

Destroyed With You is a work of fiction. Names, characters, places, and incidents are products of the author's imagination or are used fictitiously; they are not real, and any resemblance to events, establishments or persons (living or dead or undead) is entirely coincidental.

Destroyed With You Copyright © 2020 by Julie Kenner
Cover design by Michele Catalano, Catalano Creative
Cover image by Annie Ray/Passion Pages

ISBN: Digital: 978-1-949925-87-6
Print: 978-1-949925-88-3

Published by Martini & Olive Books
V-2020-12-12P

All rights reserved. No part of this book may be reproduced, scanned, or distributed in any printed or electronic form without permission. Please do not participate in or encourage piracy of copyrighted materials in violation of the author's rights. This is a work of fiction. Names, places, characters and incidents are the product of the author's imagination and are fictitious. Any resemblance to actual persons, living or dead, events or establishments is solely coincidental.

PROLOGUE

I never meant to hurt him.

I never wanted to deceive him.

I regret the past every day, but I've learned to live with remorse. With loss.

I've learned to live in the dark.

Mostly, I've learned to live without love.

Now, I hold tight to the memory of the days we had together. I hug them close, soaking in the sweet brilliance of those long-ago moments. Shared glances. Stolen kisses. Long, sunny afternoons in bed, my skin hot and slick against his.

I close my eyes and let myself go back. I ignore the pain. The loss. The grief. I cling to those moments because they are all I have. All I can ever have.

I won't ever be with him again. I know that.

Even if he wanted me—and, dear God, why would he?—I couldn't say yes.

He was in love with a woman who didn't exist. His Linda, he'd called me, but he'd been talking to a ghost. I might be flesh and blood, but I'm not real. I'm not sure I ever have been.

He's the only man who's ever made me feel whole, but I can't be with him.

Even if I had the courage to tell him my secrets, it wouldn't matter. All he would see is a woman he never knew. A woman he could never love.

Everything that had once been between us would evaporate in that moment, and where would I be then?

Still alone, but with my memories torn apart and my fantasies shattered.

At least now I can cling to the past. I can pull it out and polish it, making it shine in my memories. I can hug it hard and wish that things could have been different.

That, though, is impossible.

I can't be anything other than the woman I am.

And the stone cold truth is simple. At the end of the day, I'm not the woman he loves.

I never really was.

CHAPTER ONE

"And he really didn't tell you anything?" Emma leaned against Old Blue, Winston Starr's ancient Ford pickup.

He was Colonel Anderson Seagrave of the Sensitive Operations Command, an elite intelligence branch of the National Security Council known colloquially as the SOC. Seagrave's call had interrupted Winston while he was celebrating with his friends at Emma's sister's engagement party.

"All he said was that we needed to meet," Winston told her.

The dark night air hung thick around them. A light breeze off the ocean carried cool air toward them, but Winston didn't notice. On the contrary, he was hot. Burning from within. His mind and senses on overdrive as he turned all the possibilities over in his head, reaching one inevitable conclusion.

"But he must have mentioned Texas," she prompted. "After the call, you told me you're going back to Texas."

Winston nodded. "Tomorrow. Apparently, he'll tell me the rest when I see him tonight."

"You," Emma stressed, her hazel eyes narrowing. "Not us."

"Just me."

"You don't answer to Seagrave anymore," Emma pointed out. Once upon a time, Winston and Emma had been SOC operatives, but those days were long gone. Now they were both in the private sector, working for the Stark Security Agency, an elite organization founded by billionaire Damien Stark after the kidnapping of his youngest daughter.

"No, ma'am," Winston drawled. "I don't."

Emma scowled up at him, definitely not fooled by his supposedly casual demeanor. "If he's sending you alone, it's not about the Texas operation. By the end, our missions overlapped too much. He'd send both of us if there were lingering threads."

She frowned, then sucked in a breath as she locked eyes with him. "Linda," she said, her tone managing to be both hard and sympathetic. "It must be something to do with Linda."

His throat tightened at the sound of his wife's name, and he slid his hands in his pockets to keep them from shaking. He missed her. Even after more than four years he missed her with an intensity that bordered on pain. No, it *was* pain. A deep, potent ache that still lingered. Long after gunshots would have healed or bones knitted, he still felt it. The loss. The guilt. The stabs into his heart. The claws ripping at the fabric of his life.

His blood had drained away the night he'd lost her, and he'd been a hollow shell ever since. She'd been an innocent, caught up in something she knew nothing about.

It should have been him, dammit. If there was any true justice in the universe, it should have been him they'd killed that night.

But here he was, hale and hearty, at least on the outside. On the inside, though ... well, inside, he was as dead as she was.

He went through the motions, sure. Did his job. Laughed with his friends. But he wasn't a whole man. Not anymore. Probably never again.

As if taunting him, the sound of laughter drifted on the breeze. He glanced at the house. Emma's little bungalow was all lit up, and inside their friends continued to drink and laugh. Her sister and Quincy were getting married, after all. Proof positive that life went on.

Winston told himself that was a good thing.

Emma was waiting for him to answer, and he forced a casual shrug. "Might be somethin' else. Nothing to do with Linda at all." He heard the West Texas twang in his voice and wanted to swallow the words. He'd mostly gotten rid of the accent, but it tended to become more prominent when he was upset or confused. Or drunk.

He was a bit of all three tonight.

"Bullshit," Emma said. "You don't believe that any more than I do. You've made it perfectly clear you weren't ever going back to Texas, much less to Hades," she added, referring to the aptly named county seat where he'd served as sheriff. "He knows that. He wouldn't send you back unless it was not only important, but important to you."

Winston drew a breath, trying not to feel numb inside as he lifted his head to meet his friend and sometimes partner's eyes. "It may be nothing. Might not even be Hades."

She shook her head, the action freeing a lock of red hair from where she'd pulled it back into a messy ponytail. He could practically see the wheels turning behind those hazel eyes as she said, "I'm right. You know it. I know it. He called you at night on a weekend. This isn't a casual thing. There's a reason, and we both know what that reason is. And if you're going to Texas, then I'm going with you."

"No."

He could see her stiffen. Could practically hear

the protest before it left her lips. "Dammit, Starr. Don't do this to yourself. Remember me? I'm the one who knows you. I'm the one who was there. And I'm the one who's going to stand by you and remind you that it wasn't your goddamn fault."

"Emma, don't even—"

She held up a hand to cut off his words. "No. *No*. If you're going back there—if you're going to dredge it all up again—then you'll need a friend."

"Dredge it up?" He shook his head. "Emma, darlin', I won't be dredging anything up. It never went down in the first place."

He watched the emotions play over her face, and for a moment, he pitied her. Emma Tucker was used to getting her own way, being in command. Getting told no didn't sit well with her.

Well, too bad. He stood a little straighter and rolled his shoulders, because he wasn't backing down. Right now, she belonged right here in California with their friends. With her sister. And mostly, with Antonio Sanchez, the man she loved.

Winston hadn't had a woman in his life since Linda's death. He damn sure wasn't going to steal even a single moment of that bliss from Emma or Tony. Slowly, he reached over and placed a hand on her upper arm. "I'm going alone. And I'll be just fine."

"You're a stubborn son of a bitch."

"Funny. That's what Linda used to say." He

managed a smile and felt some of the sadness that had been pooling in his gut ease when she returned it.

"Promise you'll call. Anytime. Day or night. You need to talk—hell, you need to just sit in silence with someone else breathing—I don't care. You call."

"Well, I don't know about that," he said, cocking his head toward the open door where Tony now stood framed in the glow from inside. "Some things a man doesn't like to interrupt."

She shot him a crooked smile. "Only you, Starr. We went through hell together in Texas, and I meant what I said. You need anything, you call. Any time, day or night."

He nodded gravely, surprised by how touched he was by the ferocity in her voice. "I may take you up on that." He cocked his head toward Tony. "He know about Texas? That we knew each other before?"

"Not much. Mostly that it's where we met. That our cases overlapped."

"You tell him the rest if you want. Couples shouldn't have secrets. And you two make a good couple."

She held his gaze. "It wasn't your fault," she said again. "You were undercover. You couldn't tell her."

DESTROYED WITH YOU   9

"Oh, I could have. My mouth works just fine. I didn't. And she's dead."

"Winston, don't. You've been beating yourself up for years. You're probably black-and-blue from kicking your own ass."

He almost smiled. She wasn't wrong.

"Even if you had told her, nothing would be different. Do you think she would have left you?" Emma shook her head. "That woman adored you. She would have stayed by your side, and in the end she'd be just as dead."

She reached out and took his hand, then squeezed it hard. "It was their fault, not yours."

God, how he wanted to believe that. But all he said was, "I'm gonna get out of here now. Give Eliza a hug for me."

She sighed and dropped his hand. "You should stay."

"Probably. It would be the social thing to do. But I'm not feeling too social at the moment. And I told Seagrave I'd come by before ten."

"Winston, I—"

"Everything okay?" Tony called.

Emma turned toward him, and Winston took the opportunity to open Old Blue's door. "No," he replied before he slid behind the wheel. "I really don't think it is."

"Austin?" Winston frowned at the man seated at the battered gray table across from him. "You're sending me to Austin, not Hades?"

"Disappointed?"

Winston shook his head, trying to sort through the confused emotions running through him. "No, I —" He drew in a breath, forcing himself to lean back and look at the man who'd once been his commanding officer. "I assumed this was about Linda's death."

"Did you?" Anderson Seagrave settled back in his wheelchair, his fingers steepled under his chin. In his mid-forties, Seagrave had dark hair that was starting to gray at the temples, and an undeniable air of authority. "And what were you expecting I'd say? We brought down the Consortium years ago. Hell, you practically wrapped up that operation single-handedly."

Winston swallowed. That wasn't a time that he was proud of. He'd been so consumed by rage at Linda's murderers that he cut corners he shouldn't have, going so far as to kill Horace McNally, the man he learned had ordered her death.

That had been his breaking point. He'd been in no danger, could have easily apprehended the man. But he'd killed him instead. A single bullet to the brain. And the only regret he'd felt was that he hadn't made the bastard suffer.

Those had been harsh, messy days, and the

Consortium had been manipulating the city with murder and greed and corruption. Emma and Seagrave both told Winston that they understood. That what he'd done was justified. And that McNally would have suffered much worse in prison. McNally dabbled in child prostitution, after all. And that meant that in prison, he would have ended up somebody's bitch. Or much more painfully dead.

Winston had agreed with everything they said. He'd done right taking out that worm. But in doing so, he'd broken his own code. Broken something in *him*.

He'd retired then, leaving both the SOC and his position as sheriff, a job he'd taken as a cover in the first place, but had grown to love. He'd moved to Newport Beach for no reason other than it was Linda's favorite town. He hadn't needed to work—he'd learned after her death that Linda had a surprisingly large insurance policy on her life—and so he'd volunteered at an animal shelter, filling his days with the warm love of dogs and cats who didn't care about his failures.

His nights, though, he kept free, wanting only to be alone with his memories.

He knew he should forgive himself. After all, he hadn't killed her. The Consortium deserved the blame and his hatred. That was the cold, hard truth.

And yet he'd played a role, too. He should never have married—not when being attached to him put a target on her back. He'd been selfish, believing that their love was special. Magical. Thinking his love would keep her safe. Being selfish and stupid enough to believe that he'd die if he couldn't have her.

Well, now here he was. He didn't have her. And he was mostly dead inside. Or he had been until Seagrave had come to the shelter one day. He'd told Winston that if he truly believed he was culpable, then he should be doing something to right those wrongs. He should be back in the game, fighting the bad guys.

It had taken some soul-searching, but Winston had agreed. He'd expected to sign on with the SOC again. Instead, Seagrave introduced him to former tennis pro turned tech billionaire Damien Stark.

Stark and Ryan Hunter, Stark's friend who headed the Stark Security Agency, were the only ones in the organization who knew about Winston's connection to government intelligence operations. Even then, they didn't know he'd once been a full-on operative with the SOC. Seagrave had told them only that he'd been "attached" to the Hades investigation in his role as sheriff. Not a lie, but hardly the full truth, especially considering he'd applied for the sheriff position while officially on the books at the SOC.

Which meant that until Emma had join Stark Security, all anyone else at the SSA believed was that he'd been a small town sheriff who'd played once or twice in the big leagues before signing on with the elite organization.

That, and the painful truth that Winston had left Texas after his wife had been killed by a car bomb.

Working for Stark Security hadn't erased his pain, but it had been a balm. Now, though…

Well, now the pain and the memories had come flooding back from nothing more than the mention of Texas.

"If it's not about Linda, then what the hell is this?" He heard the edge in his voice and didn't try to tamp it down. "You just toss Texas in my face? You of all people?"

Seagrave didn't even flinch. "I said it isn't about her death," he said gravely. "At least, not exactly."

Winston frowned, too curious to be angry at his friend for what sounded like bullshit game playing. "What the hell, Anderson? Was there someone else pulling McNally's strings? Someone we missed at the top level of the Consortium? Because if there is, you point me toward the S.O.B., and I swear I will take him down in record time."

He'd spent years undercover in Hades, first landing the job, then living the role as a rural county working with the city and county officials.

The higher-ups in every office from the mayor's chambers to the police department had been corrupt down to the bone, dabbling in everything from drug-running to blackmail to massive government and civilian fraud tied to the oil and gas industry.

After Linda's death sparked that final, violent surge, the SOC and Winston had essentially shut down the spiderweb of illegal operations. As far as he knew, only two men had managed to escape the net. They'd been lower level flunkies who'd gone on to other illicit operations in other parts of the country.

One, a man who'd been known as the Serpent, was now in SOC custody thanks to Emma and Tony's latest operation. The other, Cane, was dead. And good riddance to him.

The possibility that there were other players still running free made his blood boil. He'd thought he'd burned through his fury in the passing years. Now, he knew he hadn't. The embers still glowed, ready to ignite at a moment's notice.

He drew a breath and met Seagrave's eyes. "Tell me," he demanded. "Tell me who we missed and I'll bring you his head on a platter."

"I have no doubt," Seagrave said. "But it's a little more complicated than that."

Winston sat back, eyeing the commander, trying to read what the man wasn't saying. And, more importantly, why he was dancing around the very reason that he'd called Winston in. "Then explain it to me."

"You're here because of a woman," Seagrave said flatly. His shoulders sagged as he sighed, looking older than his forty-something years. "Hell, Starr. You're here because of Linda."

Winston frowned, certain his confusion showed on his face. "You told me when I walked in here that this had nothing to do with her death."

"I didn't exactly say that. And yet, you're right. It has nothing to do with her death." He lowered his hands from the table to the wheels of his chair, then maneuvered back before rolling around the table toward Winston. Billions of dollars in government tech at his disposal, and Seagrave still preferred a manual wheelchair to one with bells, whistles, and other "gizmos," as he called them.

"Don't play games with me," Winston said. "You know better than anyone how much her death destroyed me." Emma had been transferred out soon after the bombing, so even she didn't fully know the dark pit into which he'd sunk after the forensics team positively identified Linda's DNA. Teeth. Two teeth was all they found in the bombed out shell of a car. But that had been enough to prove that the love of his life was dead.

Seagrave met his eyes, then took a remote control from a pocket on the side of his chair. He pressed a button, and a video screen whirred down from the ceiling. "I'm sorry," he said. "You're not going to like this."

Winston said nothing as the lights dimmed.

As the room darkened, the screen lit up and an image came into view. A bustling sidewalk in an urban area. Austin, maybe. Or, hell, it could be Manhattan. Seattle. Even LA. No way to tell at glance. Not from the angle of the lens focused more on the pedestrians than the surroundings.

"What are we—"

The words stuck in his throat, the answer staring him in the face.

Linda.

Oh, dear God, he was looking at his Linda.

"This is old footage," he said, his entire body going cold as fear and hope warred for dominance in his soul. "It has to be."

"It's not."

Winston's eyes locked on the screen. "When was this taken? And where?"

"Last week," Seagrave said, and Winston's stomach did a somersault. "In Seattle."

"So, you're saying what? That for some reason a government intelligence organization just happened to stumble across footage of a dead woman walking the streets of Seattle?"

"You know better than that." Now the voice was gentle.

"How long?" Winston had to clear his throat in order to continue. "Your people have had her under surveillance. Tell me how long you've known that she's alive. And then tell me why the fuck you didn't bring me in on this earlier."

"Watch."

"Dammit, Anderson, I–"

"That's an order, Starr. Watch the damn screen."

Winston watched as she entered an office building, realizing then that the footage was taken by a drone. It rose, the aspect ratio widening to take in the full Seattle skyline as it ascended higher and higher, finally hovering across the street, but level with the roof-line of the building she'd entered. The image zoomed in, focusing on a roof access shed with a closed metal door.

A few moments later, the door opened and a man stepped out. He surveyed the roof, frowned, then checked his watch.

Soon, the door opened again. At first, no one emerged, but Winston could see that the shadowy figure in the doorway was a woman. His gut constricted, and when she stepped onto the gravel and tar rooftop, he realized that he'd stopped breathing.

The man turned to her, his arms extended in greeting as he took a step toward her. Her mouth curved into a smile so familiar it made his heart

ache. His body tightened with an unfamiliar longing, then recoiled when she lifted her hand to
reveal the gun that had been concealed in the folds
of her skirt.

She aimed. She fired.

And then his Linda turned her back on the
body, slipped through the doorway, and disappeared from sight.

CHAPTER TWO

"No," Winston said, feeling sick. He shook his head, hating the weakness inside him that wished he could un-see what he'd just watched. "It's a mistake. Whatever we're looking at, it's not what it seems."

"Isn't it?"

Fury cut through Winston as he wrenched his head away from the now-dark screen to focus on Seagrave. "Why the hell did you drag me here? Haven't I been punished enough? My wife died —*died*—in a goddamn explosion. You know what I went through, damn you. You saw my pain, and you fucking sympathized. You were my friend. And now you show me this? Why? To rip me up all over again?"

"I'm showing you because you have a right to

see it. And when the shock passes, you might even thank me for bringing you the truth."

Winston huffed. "I wouldn't bet the ranch." He pushed himself out of the chair, wanting nothing more than to get out of this room and away from the nightmare playing out around him. The truth yawning before him like a dark abyss, threatening to suck him down, destroying the last, tattered remnants of joy he'd been clinging to for years.

But there wasn't any place to go. Nowhere to which he could escape. Not really.

He sank back into his chair. "Her memory is all I have left. Why the hell do you want to rip that away from me?"

Seagrave's shoulders sagged. "I'm sorry. The fact is that I need you on this. And I thought—well, I thought you'd rather curse the truth than curl up with a lie."

For the first time in over a decade, Winston wished he hadn't given up smoking. "Yeah, well, I guess you thought wrong."

"I suppose I did." Seagrave rolled toward the door. Pressing a button on the remote so that it began to swing open. "Take as long as you need. You know the way out."

Winston kept his eyes on the floor, not looking up until he heard the door click shut behind his friend. Only then did he let the tears that had been clogging his throat flow free. It couldn't be true. How the hell could it possibly be true?

Even now, he could remember the way she felt in his arms. Their long, intimate conversations. The trust they shared. The love that had filled them.

If all that was a lie, then he didn't know himself, much less his wife. He wouldn't believe that. *Couldn't* believe it. Because if it were true, then the best years of his life had been nothing but a charade. A mockery of his former happiness.

"It's not real," he told himself. "It can't be."

But of course it could. He might be trapped beneath a pain so intense he would just as soon die than work through it, but that didn't mean he was blind. Of course it could be true. He'd seen stranger things during his tenure at the SOC. And God knows he'd seen crueler women.

But his Linda? Even if it was her, how could she have walked away from him like that? She'd loved him with the same intensity that he'd loved her.

Hadn't she?

He'd never once doubted that reality, and he didn't want to now. It was as if he'd suddenly learned that gravity wasn't real, and he'd been stuck to the earth with glue all these years. It didn't feel right contemplating the possibility that she'd been playing a role. Acting a part. And yet there she was. It was her on that video—there was no doubt in his mind. And while it might be nice to think she had an identical twin or been cloned in some evil genius's laboratory, this was reality, not a Netflix series.

His wife—Linda Marie North Starr—had just killed a man in cold blood. He'd seen it, and as much as he wished he could punch Seagrave in the face and erase the whole bloody evening, he couldn't deny that basic reality. It wasn't in his nature to hide from pain or bad news, no matter how much he might want to. He had to face the truth head-on. He knew three things for certain— Linda's DNA had been recovered from the car, the body had been unrecognizable, and she'd worked for the city government of a town that was fraught with corruption.

"Damn you," he whispered as the dark threads of a twisted reality twined around him. "Don't you know I loved you?"

He took a moment to simply breathe. To calm the rage that was threatening to explode out of his fingertips. Then he stood and went to the door, planning to go find Seagrave in his office. He didn't have to. His friend was waiting in the antechamber.

"She faked her own death," Winston said.

"It certainly appears that way. I'm sorry, Winston," he added, his expression and his voice underscoring the sincerity of the words.

"I know you are," Winston said, his shoulders sagging under the weight of emotion. "So am I."

There was a battered couch against the far wall, and Winston took a seat on it. "Who was he?"

"One of ours," Seagrave said. "Deep cover with a law firm that does a significant amount of legal maneuvering for an arms dealer based in South Africa."

"She assassinated him." He had to say the words. Had to feel the weight of them on his mouth and tongue before he could believe them. "My Linda. Who once told me she didn't like me bringing my gun into the house, but that she'd get over it because of my job."

"Yes."

"Why? Who's she working for? The Consortium's gone. We ended them. Or was that fake, too?"

"As far as we know, the Consortium exists no more. We interrogated the Serpent again. He confirmed as much. As for her employer, we're still trying to ascertain who that is."

"Ascertain?" Winston scoffed. "Going easy on her, then?" His gut clenched at the thought of the interrogation techniques he imagined they were using on her. He tried to tell himself she deserved every one of them. And yet just thinking about it made him feel nauseous.

"She's not in custody," Seagrave said.

Winston stared at him, not comprehending. "You tailed her. You watched her. How the hell didn't you—?"

"That isn't our footage."

Winston leaned back in his chair, his head starting to throb. "Listen, Anderson. I get that you think I'm fragile where Linda is concerned, and maybe you're right. But spit it the fuck out, okay? Quit dancing around whatever you know and whatever you want me to do. Tell me now, or I'm walking."

Seagrave moved closer. "Here it is, then. That wasn't her first kill. Not by a long shot. And we have intel that she has a new assignment. I need you, Winston. You're the best man for this job."

"Am I?" His voice was rough. His body numb.

"You know her better than anyone. We need to stop the coming assassination. And we want to bring her in alive."

He studied Seagrave's face. "You're saying she's a professional, but you think she'll falter if it's me she's up against. That I can bring her in alive where nobody else can."

Seagrave lifted a shoulder.

"I have a job."

"And I've spoken with both Ryan and Damien. I told them I wanted to borrow you for a special assignment."

"They don't know I used to work for you."

"They still don't," Seagrave assured him. "But they do believe that you've had joint operations with the SOC before. I told them I need you on special assignment. And I told them why."

"You told them about Linda. About that video."

"No. But I told them you'd want to be involved."

"I *don't* want to be involved."

"No?"

Winston pushed up off the couch and paced to the window. He looked down at Los Angeles a dozen floors beneath them. "Don't play mind games with me, Colonel. You'll only piss me off."

Behind him, Seagrave sighed. "That isn't my intent. If you truly want to walk away, I won't pressure you. But I don't think that you do."

Winston closed his eyes, working to keep his whole body from sagging with the truth of that statement. He told himself he wanted nothing more than to go home and forget he heard any of this. To let some other agent go in and learn why Linda had killed that man. Why she'd killed others, too, assuming what Seagrave said was true. He should use this meeting as a fulcrum. A lever to send his past life with Linda tumbling down into a pile of so much rubble, and a springboard to move on with his life.

Not gonna happen.

He turned back. "Whatever she's involved in, it's not what you think. She's innocent."

Seagrave's expression didn't change. "I hope you're right. I don't think you are. But I like that you're playing Devil's advocate."

"And what exactly is the assignment? If you want me to take her out, I won't do it." For that matter, he'd actively foil anyone who tried. He wanted—*needed*—answers. And no one was touching her until he had them.

"I want you to apprehend her before she eliminates her target. Then I want you to bring her and the target in safely. Along with the laptop the target will have with him."

"The target's in Austin?" Winston asked, shifting into professional mode. Tamping down the emotions that could keep him from doing his job. And, dammit, he was going to do it. No way was someone else going into the field to confront her. "When is she supposed to make the hit? For that matter, how do you know any of this?"

Seagrave didn't answer. Instead, he lifted the remote and started the video running again. "Since receiving the footage you saw, we've been able to confirm that Linda Starr—who now goes by Michelle Moon—is responsible for at least two other assassinations of high level agents that we know of. And we suspect she's behind several others."

"Michelle Moon," he repeated, his voice like sandpaper.

"Does that mean something to you?"

"No," Winston lied. "Not a damn thing."

Seagrave studied him, but didn't pursue the comment. "This man," he said, pausing on the image on the face of a clean-shaven man with thinning brown hair. "Our intel suggests that he's her next target. He arrived in Austin yesterday and is scheduled to stay for a week. Tommy Bartlett."

Winston frowned. "What's the goal here? Apprehending Linda? Bartlett? Or is this about whatever's on that computer?"

Seagrave smiled at Winston as if he'd just aced his final exam. "I'd say that just about covers it."

Winston frowned, but didn't push. Seagrave would reveal what he wanted to reveal. *Need to know*. The buzzwords of their profession.

"I will say this—we want that computer. But even so, all sides of the triangle are equal."

"I'll keep that in mind," Winston said. "But can't you just hack the machine? I've seen the brainpower employed by the SOC, not to mention the resources Stark has, and we both know you utilize Stark International's tech departments."

"Would that we could. It's completely old school. The only way to access the information is to sit in front of that machine—then get past all the protections, which are apparently rigged with self-destruct traps. That machine gets the biometric information or the wrong password or gets broken or lost, and we lose a lot of valuable information. Which is why we want the man, too. What's in his head is valuable as well."

Winston took a moment to process everything. "Tell me this—why me? You've got solid intel. Send in a team and bring her in. The accountant, too. How hard can that be? And then here I am to help with the interrogation."

"Too risky. If we pull Bartlett, she goes into the wind. This is the first time we've had a solid lead on her location ahead of a hit. We want her, Starr. Surely you can understand that."

He swallowed. "Yeah. I get it."

"If we put a tail on her target, we have to assume she'll get wind of it and go under."

Winston leaned back, studying Seagrave's face. He had to hand it to the man—there were no clues. Still, Winston thought he understood the situation. "Bartlett's one of ours, too, isn't he? A deep cover operative. You think whoever she's working for has managed to get his hands on a list of undercover agents. You call in a team—hell, you call in anyone who officially works at the SOC—and you risk tipping them off. I'm not the best man for the job because my wife's picking your boys off. I'm the best man because I don't belong to you anymore."

"And because you're so damn smart," Seagrave

said, with just the slightest hint of a smile. "Although you're wrong about Bartlett being an agent. He's not. He's a civilian in the employee of a man named Billy Hawthorne. Do you know the name?"

"Should I?"

"McNally's heir apparent," Seagrave said, his voice grave.

Winston's mouth went dry. "What are you saying? We took down the Consortium."

"We did. Hell, *you* did. Billy surfaced about a year ago. He's McNally's nephew, and apparently he's decided to resurrect the family business. Or some version of it, anyway."

"Fuck."

"That's pretty much the entire intelligence community's take on the situation."

Winston cracked a smile. "And you're hoping to nip it in the bud before his organization gets as powerful as his role model's."

"Got it in one."

"Which is how Bartlett fits in," Winston said.

Seagrave nodded. "He's this close to agreeing to testify for us," he added, holding his thumb and forefinger just millimeters apart. "He's key. The information on that computer is even more important."

"What did he witness? Murder?"

A hint of a smile touched Seagrave's lips. "No,

but you could say he knows where the bodies are buried. And who buried them. He's an accountant for Hawthorne's operation."

"An accountant?"

"Not sexy, but it was accounting that took down Capone. People forget that."

Winston nodded in understanding. Bartlett had access to books and information that could put his employer behind bars, and that employer wanted to eliminate the risk. And Linda was hired to be the ax man. To take out a witness so that the masterminds of a criminal empire could go free.

"In Bartlett's case, it's not just the financials. It's who he was doing the work for."

"Explain."

"Bartlett works with one of our covert organizations. His handler is Dustin Collins, one of the operational commanders in ID-9."

"ID-9?"

"Intelligence Division Nine. The ID protocol was funded about the time you joined the SOC. The agents assigned to the various ID sections have even deeper cover. Longer term assignments."

"Why is the SOC bringing in an ID-9 witness?"

"We're not."

Winston frowned, waiting for Seagrave to tell him the rest.

"Bartlett's agreed to testify against both Hawthorne and Collins."

"Collins?" Winston let out a slow whistle. "An operational commander is dirty?"

"I've been watching him for a while. Oversight of the ID divisions falls to the SOC."

Winston's blood ran cold. "So you're positive Collins is a mole?"

"I am," Seagrave said. "And we have the chance to nail him with Bartlett's testimony and the evidence on the laptop. Which means you need to bring him in. I need Bartlett alive. I need Linda alive. And I need that machine."

Winston studied his friend's face. "You told me about Linda so that I'd take this assignment."

"I told you about Linda because you have a right to know," Seagrave countered. "But knowing what you do, I think you can empathize with the depth of Collins' betrayal."

Shit.

"Well?" Seagrave pressed.

No matter how much he might want to bury his head in the sand for this one, he couldn't. Not for something as important as this.

"Agent," Seagrave said, though Winston wasn't officially an agent anymore. "Will you take this assignment?"

Winston shifted, looking back at the screen. The video had played past the image of Bartlett, returning to Linda standing on the roof, the gun in her hand. She was frozen there, and Winston was sure that Seagrave had the tech boys edit that shot right onto the end of the footage. A final punch to push him over the edge if he was undecided.

He wasn't.

"I'm in," he said. "Never thought I'd say this, but I guess I'm going back to Texas."

CHAPTER THREE

"You're sure it won't be a problem?" Winston shifted in the chair across from Ryan Hunter's desk. Problem or not, he was going to Texas. But he preferred to go with Hunter's blessing.

"Special loan to the SOC," Hunter said. He lifted his hands in a *what can you do?* gesture. "How can I compete with that?"

"Well, I appreciate it," Winston said. Ryan Hunter headed up Stark Security, answering only to billionaire Damien Stark who, as far as Winston had been able to tell, let Hunter take the lead where the agency was concerned. In existence for only a few years, the SSA had already earned its reputation as a force to be reckoned with both domestically and internationally.

"You're an asset, Starr," Ryan said. "If the SOC

is trying to poach you, we're going to be butting heads. But if Seagrave just needs you on loan for an operation, that's not a problem." A half-smile danced over his lips. "I'm more than happy for covert intelligence organizations to owe us favors."

He leaned forward, his arms crossed on his desk as he studied Winston. "I'll admit I'm curious. I won't ask you to break any confidences, but can you tell me what this is about?"

"Not really." In truth, he probably could have told Hunter that his dead wife had reappeared and he'd been tasked with figuring out what the hell was going on. Seagrave trusted both Stark and Hunter, and he'd understand that Winston needed someone to talk to.

Except, of course, he didn't need someone. Or maybe he did, but he wasn't going to take the comfort. Not when revealing the situation would also reveal the possibility that he'd been an idiot. Practically a cuckold. Used by his wife for some nefarious purpose he still didn't understand. She'd betrayed him—he knew that. No matter how much he wanted to protest that it was all a misunder-standing, he knew better. She'd used him—and then when she was done with him, she'd slipped off into the dark, ensuring that he wouldn't follow by making him believe she was dead.

He'd been a lovesick fool, and that wasn't some-thing he was inclined to share with the man who not only signed his paycheck, but who trusted Winston's instincts in the field. And, honestly, he didn't want to see the look of sympathy on his friends' faces once they learned the truth. Which was why he intended to hold this particular truth very close to the vest.

"I can't share the details," he told Hunter. "But it ties back to my days as sheriff. You already know I spent some time working closely with the SOC back then."

"A new player's popped up in an old case," Hunter said. "I understand. You'll be missed, but we'll make do. I'll pair Leah with Renly while you're away. Let her help him get settled."

"Renly?"

Hunter shook his head, frowning. "Sorry, Renly Cooper. I forgot you weren't there last night. He dropped by Emma's place after you left."

"I look forward to meeting him."

"He's in with Sarah if you want to say hello." Sarah was the former part-time office manager who'd recently been bumped to full-time.

"When I get back," Winston said, glancing at his watch. "I'm flying commercial and need to run if I'm going to make my plane."

"Austin, right?"

"Not a bad location for an assignment." He tried to look casual. In truth, he'd always loved the capital city of Texas. He hadn't been back since

Linda's death—or, rather, since her betrayal. It had been their favorite weekend getaway, and the thought of going without her had been too much to bear.

Now she was alive, and he was going back to apprehend her, and he was certain that this would be the last time he'd visit that city. No matter how this ended, his memories—and Austin—would be tainted.

"I'm sure the SOC has you well-equipped, and since I don't know the mission, I can't speak to specifics. But you should meet up with Noah Carter when you get there."

"Will do," he said, taking the card Ryan proffered. He'd met Noah once before at one of Stark's functions. A post-Grammy Award party in honor of popular singer Kiki King, Noah's wife. In the past, Noah had worked with a shadowy vigilante group called Deliverance, several members of which were now working for Stark Security.

A tech genius, Noah had left Deliverance to run the Austin office of Stark Applied Technology. Winston couldn't think of any specific tech he required, but who knew what he might need on the fly, and he had a feeling that Noah possessed the kind of backend hacker skills that might come in handy.

"I'll give him a call from the road," Winston promised. "Buy him lunch once I get there." With the time change, he'd be arriving around two, so it would be a late lunch. And after that, he'd need to get in place to intercept Linda.

He turned when he heard the light tap at the door. Leah smiled at him, her brows rising above her black glasses. "I'm heading out if you want me to drop you at the airport. Unless you've already called a rideshare?"

"A lift would be great."

"Have a good trip," Hunter said, rising as Winston did. "Don't hesitate to call if you need anything."

"What would you need?" Leah asked as they headed for the main doors. "Isn't this a family thing?"

Winston felt a twinge of guilt for telling her that. They'd worked closely for his entire tenure at Stark Security. Hell, they'd even gotten drunk in Hong Kong together, then managed to get completely lost as they stumbled back to their hotel. If he'd had any doubt as to Leah's friendship or her value as a partner, those doubts had been erased when she'd not only managed to guide them in a blind stupor, but had never breathed a word to anyone at Stark Security about their lapse in judgment.

True, the case had already been resolved, and they'd stayed an extra day to play tourist. But Winston didn't usually drink that much, and certainly not in a foreign country. He'd seen a woman though—a woman who'd reminded him of Linda. And damned if he hadn't been gutted.

He pressed his fingers to his temples as the memory of his monster headache returned. Not only that, but as a sick sense of dread rose in him. He'd gotten blind drunk because of a glimpse of a stranger. How the hell did he expect to survive this mission if he was chasing the real woman?

"Earth to Winston," she said as he grabbed his duffel off his desk and slung it over his shoulder.

"What? Oh, sorry. Yes. A family thing."

"I thought so." She rummaged in her purse. "Oh, hell. Hang on. I'll be back in a sec."

He watched as she headed toward Sarah's office, his mind still with his parents. They lived in Llano, a pretty little town in the Hill Country. They were retired now and had bought a small movie theater with their savings. His brother and sister-in-law helped them run it, and Winston was impressed that, so far at least, they hadn't lost their shirts. Then again, his father had bought stock in Google and Microsoft and Netflix before any of the companies had exploded. So he'd been able to retire as a criminal defense attorney in favor of a job that let him air classic movies like *Twelve Angry Men* and *Witness for the Prosecution*.

He talked to his parents regularly, but he hadn't seen them in ages. He'd vowed to never return to

Texas after Linda had died, but he'd always known that vow couldn't apply to his family. Eventually he'd have buried enough of the pain to justify a visit when he wouldn't be a numb husk of a man. And Llano was a long way from Hades.

Now, he almost wished he had more time before he had to be in Austin. It would be good to sit and talk with his dad and have his mom fuss over him and tell him he didn't eat enough.

That's how it was before. Now, though ... well, now he hadn't been home for over three years. He'd gone to see them after Linda's death. After he'd killed McNally and had needed to heal. It had helped. And yet at the same time it hadn't. Because staring at his parents—at their tight relationship and the way they could read each other's thoughts and anticipate each other's needs—God, it had reminded him so much of Linda he'd almost been unable to breathe.

He'd spent the entire trip feeling like a vacuum, sucking in their sympathy and giving nothing back.

Now, damn him, he wanted his mother's comfort and his father's gentle wisdom. But he knew damn well that he wouldn't go. They'd loved her, too. They'd mourned for the woman they'd believed she was, and he wasn't going to taint their memories with the truth.

But it's not the truth. There's some other explanation. There must be.

The words whispered through his mind, but he knew better. There might be a twist in the last chapter of every crime novel he read, but life didn't work that way. The reality you saw was the reality that existed, and you either learned to adapt or you died.

Once upon a time, he had wanted to die. Going on without her had been too heavy a load to bear. And then last night—the revelation she'd faked her death had knocked the wind out of him all over again.

But it hadn't broken him. Not this time.

If anyone was about to be broken, it was Linda, not him. And while he hated the circumstances, he couldn't deny the warm call of the rage inside him that wanted nothing more than to bring her down.

"You were in there a while," he said, when Leah returned.

"Sorry. I left my keys on Sarah's desk, but then I got talking to Renly. He has some seriously great stories."

Winston glanced toward the glass walls of Sarah's office where Renly Cooper sat with a hip on her desk as she flipped through paperwork, probably to make sure all the various contracts and confidentiality agreements were signed.

"Navy SEAL," Winston said. "I suppose he would have good stories."

"Oh, yeah, I guess he has some good SEAL

stories, too," Leah said as they headed toward the elevator that would take them to the basement parking area. "I hadn't really thought about that. Then again, our Stark Security stories are probably just as good."

"Then what are you talking about?"

She pressed the button to call the elevator then turned to gape at him. "Don't you know who he is?"

"I would say Renly Cooper, but I have a feeling that's not the answer you're looking for."

"You really are a Luddite. Do you even have a Facebook account? Or Twitter?"

"I don't," he said. "And yet somehow I manage to soldier on."

He could almost see the effort she made not to roll her eyes.

"He just broke up with Marissa McQuire," she said instead. "And before that, he was dating Francesca Muratti. He's the reason their friendship went all to hell."

"I didn't realize it had. Then again, I didn't know they were friends."

She narrowed her eyes. "You don't even know who I'm talking about, do you?"

He rattled off both women's most recent films. "I like cinema," he said. "Pretty sure that doesn't mean I have to like Hollywood gossip, too."

This time, she really did roll her eyes. "Sometimes the gossip is more entertaining than the movie."

"Well, you may be right there. So who is he that he knows these women? He comes from a Hollywood family?"

"He consults on movies. Isn't that cool? He was doing it full-time, but then he met Damien at a party or something, and I guess he's looking for something with a bit more meaning. Honestly, I don't know all of it. But he seems nice."

Winston shot her a glance over the roof of the car before they both slipped inside. "Well, enjoy the next few days showing him the ropes. Just don't enjoy it too much."

She scowled, then started the car. "I said he's interesting, not that I'm spreading my legs."

He laughed. That was one of the things he loved about Leah. One minute she could be as bouncy as a teen, the next she was as crude as a hooker. She was one of their best undercover operatives, and it was in part because of that chameleon blood.

"I stand corrected," he said. "I thought I'd caught the whiff of a crush on you."

"I'll cop to suffering under the weight of unrequited attraction," she admitted. "But Renly Cooper is not the object of my desire."

"Is it serious?"

She laughed. "Not even close."

He nodded sagely. "Just as well. Less likely to get hurt if you take it slow."

"Did you and Linda?"

He tensed and hoped she didn't notice. He and Leah had spent long hours on assignments together and she knew how much he'd loved—and missed—his wife. But there was no way for her to know that Linda was the last person he wanted to talk about right now, even if she was the only person filling his thoughts.

"No," he said with a half-smile. "We didn't take it slow at all. We both fell hard and fast. And in the end," he added as he turned toward her, "the hurt cut deep."

"I know," she said. "But that was different."

"Yeah," he said, realizing she spoke more truly than she knew. "Very different."

CHAPTER FOUR

"So tell me how I can help." Noah Carter lifted his glass, then took a sip of beer. "Ryan didn't tell me a thing other than that you might reach out. Anderson told me a bit more."

"Did he?"

Noah shrugged. "Ryan told me you were coming and might need tech. It wasn't for an SSA mission, so I called Anderson. Asked if he knew you and what was up."

"Huh," Winston said.

"Impressed or annoyed?" Noah's question was highlighted by a grin.

"Of all the possibilities, you pulled the SOC out of your ass? I guess that makes me impressed."

"Honestly, it wasn't that hard to figure."

"Wasn't it?"

The other man leaned back, his clean-shaven

face amused. "Now you're just fishing for trade secrets. But that's fair. You're in the trade, after all." He polished off the rest of his beer and signaled to the waitress for another round. "You work for Stark Security, and I happen to know that the SSA has a good relationship with not only Anderson Seagrave, but with the SOC in general."

Winston nodded. That was true. Not only had he and Emma both worked for the covert government agency, but so had Denny's husband Mason and Denny herself. It was worthwhile work, that was for damn sure, but they'd all paid harsh prices for their time-served.

"Go on," he urged.

Noah pulled a french fry out of the basket they were sharing. They'd met at The Fix on Sixth, a local bar on Austin's Sixth Street, a short walk from both Noah's office and the Stark Century Hotel where, according to the intel, Bartlett had checked in about an hour before.

"Ryan wouldn't breach confidence. If he suggested you reach out to me, it was because he had authority. And the only covert agency that Ryan knows I work with is the SOC."

"But it's not the only covert agency you work with," Winston said, amused.

"What's that parable? If you build it, they will come. I've got a long list of comers at my door. And so long as neither me nor Damien have an issue with their particular way of doing business, all currency is equal."

"That's very capitalist of you."

Noah laughed. "Yeah? My wife says it's vanity. Seeding my tech out into the world. Maybe, but my products still aren't as far reaching as her songs."

"I've got all her albums," Winston admitted. "She's talented."

Noah's smiled with such pride it made Winston's heart ache. "She really is."

"From what I'm learning, so are you. Maybe more so than Ryan intimated. Tell me the rest of it."

The waitress arrived with their second round, and Noah lifted his in a toast. Winston did the same as Noah said, "Like Carmac the Magnificent, I will reveal all I know about you and yours."

"I'm breathless with anticipation. What else did Anderson tell you? And what have you figured out on your own?"

"Only that your mission was important. You're here to recover evidence from a potential witness named Bartlett and possibly stop a contract killer."

"That about sums it up."

"The killer's a woman, I'm guessing. Ex-girl-friend or partner. Maybe wife. Definitely someone you used to sleep with."

Winston managed not to choke on his drink. "Christ, Noah. You really do deserve that turban."

"Nah. It's just basic logic." He grinned, full of

self-confidence. Well-deserved, apparently. "First off, the SOC has a branch office in Austin. There's no shortage of agents and yet they sent you all the way from LA. Second, it's just you. Not a team, which suggests to me that it's either a highly confidential assignment or they want her taken alive. Or both."

He met Winston's eyes, as if to say *how am I doing so far?*

"Go on."

"I think it's fair to assume she's dangerous, and that means they sent you—as opposed to some other solo SOC operative—because there's a high likelihood that she'll keep you alive, whereas with someone else, she'll go balls to the wall to escape.

"In other words," he continued, in the tone of someone taking a sweeping bow, "they're banking that because of either guilt or nostalgia that she'll either decide to come quietly or she'll falter. Either way, you're the best man for the job." He leaned back. "So, how'd I do?"

"Hunter told me you were a tech genius. Seems to me he could have left out the tech part."

Noah laughed. "Appreciate the compliment." His brow furrowed. "So who is she to you? Former partner?"

"Something like that," Winston admitted, not sure why he was opening up to this near-stranger. "She was my wife."

"Christ."

Winston shrugged, as if to say it was no big deal, when, of course, it was everything. "Once upon a time, she was my world, and I thought I was hers. Apparently, I couldn't have been more wrong."

Noah nodded slowly, and a shadow seemed to cross his face as he said, "Can I give you a piece of advice?"

"Sure."

"I've seen a lot. Experienced a lot. And the only thing I'm certain of is that things are often not what they seem." He took a long swallow of beer. "Just food for thought."

Winston thought back to the video that Seagrave had shown him, wishing that what Noah just said would turn out to be true, but at the same time certain that it wouldn't.

"So, tell me what I can do for you specifically. I'm happy to load up your saddlebags with tech, but I need a sense of what you need."

"For one thing you can get me access to Bartlett's room."

"Well, hell," Noah said. "I was hoping for a challenge." He reached into his suit coat pocket and pulled out a card key. "I thought you might ask that. He's in three-twelve. That's a master. Do me a favor and don't bother any other guests. I'd rather not have to explain to Mr. Stark."

"Done," Winston promised.

"You could nab him now, you know."

Winston nodded. "But that increases the risk that I won't get the woman. The SOC wants them both." And he wanted Linda.

"Makes sense. You'll be interested to know he has a table in the bar booked for six-fifteen. A two-top."

"Does he? That is interesting."

"I thought it might be. Either it's a business meeting, or he has a date. Either way, I bet it's your girl."

Winston nodded. He'd been thinking the exact same thing. Based on what Seagrave said, the information on that laptop had significant value. Bartlett was cooperating with the government—at least he appeared to be. But if he was the kind of guy who did business with the Horace McNallys and Billy Hawthornes of the world, then he was undoubtedly the kind of man who would sell information for his own profit before he let the government wring him dry for free.

"Want me to work this with you?" Noah asked. "Not in person, obviously, but I can be on comms."

Winston considered. There was some comfort in knowing someone would have his back, ready to send the cavalry in if everything went horribly wrong. But he shook his head. For one, the SOC wanted this to be a solo operation—*his* solo operation. More importantly, he didn't want his hands tied. Comms meant accountability. And from the moment he'd learned the truth about Linda's betrayal, something dark inside of him had reared its head. He wanted time alone with her. To question her without an audience. To learn, once and for all, what had gone wrong between them.

Still, he hated to turn down assistance. "I need to run solo on this one, and you've already helped beyond measure just getting me access to Bartlett's room."

"I can do more."

"Not on comms," Winston said. "I don't need you in my ear. But how about an amplifier? If it is my target he's meeting in the bar, I want to hear what they say. But I'm not in a position to grab the table next to them."

"Far enough away to go unnoticed and unrecognized," Noah said. "And that's too far to eavesdrop without assistance."

"Exactly."

Once again, Noah smiled. "I think I can load you up." He lifted a hand, signaling for the check. "My office is just a few blocks away. Let's go see what toys we can find."

CHAPTER FIVE

Winston had to hand it to Damien Stark— the Stark Century Hotel in Austin had one of the nicest bars he'd ever been in. And Winston had been in quite a few. Then again, he'd come to know Stark pretty well, and he wouldn't have expected anything less.

What made this particular bar so impressive was the way that it seamlessly fit his needs for the evening. Unlike some hotel bars that were geared for a raucous after-work crowd, the Library Bar was designed to promote a calmer feel. Lush leather chairs surrounded dark wooden tables. Bookcases filled with modern and classical literature lined the walls. And dim lighting enhanced the library theme, with most of the illumination coming from the brass reading lamps that accented each table.

The actual bar attracted a few who stood and

flirted, but on the whole the room was quiet and dignified—and dark enough to allow the clientele to slip into anonymity.

Winston tried to do just that. Because of his connection to all things Stark, Noah had been able to tell him the exact table that Bartlett had reserved, and Winston had selected a seat on the curve of the oval shaped bar. The location had several advantages. If he shifted on the stool, he had line-of-sight to Bartlett's table. But when he sat casually, all that anyone in that area would see was his back.

He had Noah's tech to help him out, too. A simple receiver already in his ear, and a multidirectional microphone built into the earpiece of the glasses he wore as camouflage. Plus, he could shift the direction of the mic simply by manipulating the controls on his phone.

Anyone looking his way would assume he was nothing more than a businessman having a solo drink and scrolling through emails.

Of course, there was some risk that Linda would recognize him. But in Hades, he'd tended to live in either jeans or his Sheriff's uniform. In all their time together, she probably saw him in a suit less than half-a-dozen times. And that was counting their wedding.

And this suit ... hell, he might as well have bought a small car. He'd picked it out from the

DESTROYED WITH YOU   53

men's store in the lobby of the hotel. A silk and wool blend, it was about as high end as a suit could be without being custom made. And even then, the tailor had managed to make the alterations within an hour. The price tag had almost given him a heart attack, but he'd charged it to the SOC, thank you very much. This mission might be eating him alive, but at least he'd look damn good while suffering.

He looked different, too, for that matter. At least from Linda's perspective. His face was slightly more tan these days, simply from the fact that he lived by the beach now. Between long walks and the weekends he spent on his small boat, he got more sun than he had from beneath the broad brim of a sheriff's hat, even in the brutal Texas summers.

Not that he was wearing a hat now. But his hair had changed as well. Shorter and worn close to his scalp. Less trouble and fewer memories. Linda had liked to run her fingers through his hair as they'd snuggled close in bed talking, and it had been cathartic to shear away the hair even if he couldn't seem to lose the memories.

He'd had a beard then, too. Not much of one, but more than just a day-old shadow. Now, he was clean-shaven.

All minor changes, but they added up. Even Noah had agreed when Winston had shown him a photo from the Texas years. "If she looks hard, she'll recognize you. But I doubt she'll look hard at anyone but Bartlett."

The statement had both reassured Winston and depressed him. He wanted the camouflage, sure. But the idea that the woman who had been his entire life wouldn't even recognize him was like a kick in the gut.

Then again, he didn't recognize her, either. Physically, sure—at least he recognized her easily enough in the video. But the woman she was now? A woman who could so easily point a gun, fire, and then just walk away to leave the body to rot on a rooftop? He didn't know that woman at all.

"Will someone be joining you?" The smooth voice of the hostess filled Winston's head, and he turned down the volume on his earpiece as Bartlett replied.

"Yes. She should be—oh. There she is now."

Winston couldn't help it; he had to turn. He shifted just enough to look over his shoulder, then immediately regretted the impulse.

His heart had twisted when he'd seen her in the video, but that had been more from what she was doing than what she looked like. Seeing her now, in the flesh, it felt as if he was being flayed alive.

She stood by the hostess stand, her honey-blonde hair falling loose around her shoulders. She wore a pale pink dress with a fitted bodice and a skirt that hinted at the shape of her thighs as she walked toward the table, her eyes on Bartlett and her smile wide.

The smile she'd once aimed at him.

God, how could he have been so stupid?

"You look amazing," Bartlett said, standing. He didn't, however, pull out her chair. Linda would notice that.

Winston grimaced, frustrated with himself. This wasn't about a jilted ex watching his wife go out with a new man. This was about averting a hit and recovering the laptop. And Winston would do well to keep that in mind.

"It's wonderful to see you again," she said, putting down a leather tote as she sat. Her voice felt like a low, sensual purr in Winston's ear. "I was afraid you'd turn me down."

"Not a chance." Bartlett cleared his throat. "Well, okay, actually, yeah. I almost didn't call you back. I'm not a stupid man, and pissing off Billy Hawthorne would be the epitome of stupid."

He could hear the trill of her sweet laughter even without the comm. He'd always loved the way she laughed, and he had to force himself to turn away, knowing that he'd already looked too long and risked too much. Instead, he focused on the bourbon in front of him, swirling the glass and watching as the single ice cube began to melt while their conversation filled his head.

"Billy and I are just friends," she said. "But I

think he noticed the way I was looking at you, because when I told him I was coming to Austin for a work thing, he mentioned that you'd be here, too. And, well, that was too happy a coincidence to pass up. I hope you don't think I was too bold calling you like that?"

Winston rolled his eyes as Bartlett's voice cracked with his reply. "Oh, no. I—I mean, it was great to hear from you."

"I'm so glad." Her voice was low and intimate, and Winston had to force himself to relax before he cracked the whiskey glass he was holding.

"You're from here originally, aren't you?" Bartlett asked. "Texas, I mean. I hear a little bit of an accent."

"I lived in West Texas when I was younger." Her voice was flat, almost clipped.

"Do you miss it?" Bartlett asked, and Winston decided the guy was an idiot. Or at least too head-over-heels to actually pay attention to the signals she was giving off.

"No," she said curtly. "To be honest, I try not to think about it at all."

At the bar, Winston closed his eyes. That, he supposed, was something they still had in common. He didn't like to think about his years in Texas either.

"I wouldn't have even come to Austin if it hadn't been necessary," she continued, and despite himself, Winston smiled. That was two things.

"Oh." Bartlett cleared his throat, apparently realizing he'd hit a sore spot. "So, where do you live?"

"Chicago," she said. "Not far from Billy, actually. We met at a charity fundraiser."

"Right. He's, um, very civic-minded."

For a moment, there was nothing but the clatter of silverware and the hum of ambient conversation coming through the receiver in Winston's ear. He was about to turn and sneak another quick glance when Linda cleared her throat.

"Would you be upset if I said I don't want to talk about Billy Hawthorne?" Her voice was as smooth as honey. The same voice that had urged Winston into bed so many nights. That had soothed him when he'd come home frustrated because something had gone wrong, either in the Sheriff's department or in his real job fighting the Consortium. That sweet lilt. That sensual tone. Never once had it failed to compel him. To melt him.

Tonight, all it did was anger him. Because it had all been a lie, just as much as her flirting with Bartlett was a lie. She was here to kill Bartlett, after all. And though Winston might still be walking, she'd killed him, too, a long time ago.

The sound of Bartlett's chuckle rang in

Winston's ear. "Trust me. While I'm sitting across from you, talking about Billy Hawthorne is the last thing I want to do."

For a moment, she was silent. Then, very softly, she said, "I'm glad to hear that."

Winston couldn't stay still any longer. He turned just enough to see her reach for his hand. The intimate caress set rage and grief warring inside him. But it was the ring she wore that confirmed what Seagrave had told him and sent a wave of nausea crashing through him.

A large ring, almost gaudy, with a single stone set in platinum. He couldn't see it from his perspective, but if he were closer, Winston knew he'd see the snake etched into the gem.

Lovely and ornate, but also dangerous.

He'd seen that ring before. In Hades. Then, it had been on the finger of a stacked blonde who'd come on to Winston in a bar, and though he'd been vocal in his disinterest, she'd managed to slide her hand along his neck. He'd felt the prick, but by that time it had been too late.

Fortunately, Emma had been working with him that night. She'd taken the bitch down as Winston fought to stay conscious.

He'd been lucky. The hidden needle in the ring had held only a sedative. But it could have just as easily been poison.

Now Linda had the same ring. And the only

good that he could see coming from that was the fact that any lingering doubts were now soundly swept away. This was no wacky coincidence, no unfortunate misinterpretation of facts.

His wife wasn't just dead; she'd never existed.

And knowing that made it a hell of a lot easier to do his job.

He'd bring her in. And if it came down to him or her, he'd kill her without a moment's hesitation.

"Are you staying here?" Linda asked, and though Winston couldn't see her, he knew Bartlett must have nodded affirmatively because she whispered, all sultry and sweet, "Oh, that's very good."

"You, um, you think so?"

"Well, it's a very nice hotel. I've been to the bar and restaurant a few times, but I've never seen one of the rooms. I'm guessing they're exceptional."

"Oh, yes. Very nice." Bartlett cleared his throat noisily. "If you—I mean, we could have wine and appetizers sent to the room. Maybe, um, order a movie."

"I love that idea," she said. "But Tommy, I don't think we need to waste money on a movie we'll just end up ignoring, do you? I mean, unless you like background noise."

As Tommy Bartlett cleared his throat and probably blushed like a teenager, Winston closed his eyes, not sure if he was battling shock or disgust or something far more disturbing. Like arousal. When they'd been together he'd always taken the lead in their sex life. But he couldn't deny that he'd often fantasized about her seducing him in his office or slamming him hard against the entryway wall the moment he got home at the end of the day, ignoring his protests that he was exhausted, and then going down on him right there in the front hall.

He'd never told her about those thoughts. God knows their sex life had been plenty fine, and he'd always feared she'd feel obligated to try and be something she wasn't if he confessed his fantasies.

Now, he wasn't sure which was the real Linda.

Neither, he assumed. She was playing a role now with Bartlett just as she'd played one with him.

She was a chameleon, and the only way he was going to manage not to lose his grip during this assignment was if he kept that basic fact firmly at the forefront of his mind.

"—take the check?"

Winston grimaced, realizing that he'd tuned out the conversation. He kept his back to them as he tossed a fifty on the bar, more than covering his own bill, then he headed out, certain they'd soon be following.

It was easy enough to get to Bartlett's room. He

had the number from Noah as well as a master key, and he moved quickly since he was certain that Bartlett would be eager to get Linda to the room before she changed her mind.

But once he reached the actual door, he moved with more care. Bartlett might be an accountant, but he was an accountant who did the bulk of his work for criminals.

Winston checked the door for any threads or micro-wires that might have been put in place in order to reveal if anyone had opened the door despite the Do Not Disturb sign. Nothing.

So far so good. He pressed the key against the pad, heard the lock click, then entered slowly. He was almost certain the room would be empty, but he wasn't about to leave anything up to chance.

Silence greeted him, and he saw no suggestion of another person. Only a suitcase open on a stand and a magazine tossed on the bed. Simple indicators of one guy, not intending to stay too long.

But there was no laptop sitting out.

Winston frowned. Bartlett hadn't had the computer with him in the bar, of that much he was certain. The man had been wearing trousers and a button down, and he'd carried no briefcase. If there'd been even the slightest chance that the man had the laptop with him, Winston wouldn't have come ahead to the room. Linda already had the accountant wrapped around her finger. If Bartlett had brought the laptop to the bar, she would have suggested they go to her hotel. Someplace where she had all the control.

Unless the laptop wasn't here, either...

The thought made Winston frown, then glance at his watch. They might already be on their way, but he needed to know. He shot a quick text to Noah, who responded almost immediately, assuring Winston that Bartlett hadn't stored a laptop in the hotel vault, nor was there one logged in with the bellmen.

He also gave Winston the override code for the guest safe located in the closet. But before Winston could access that vault, he heard the snick of the lock on the door. He eased all the way into the closet and carefully slid the door closed. The panel was louvered, giving him a striated view of the room. And the bed.

"Oh, this really is nice." Linda's voice preceded her into the room, and Winston stiffened, stepping back as they passed in front of the door. "I'm so glad you invited me up."

Bartlett was laughing as he stepped into view. "Funny. I could have sworn you invited yourself up."

"Oh, did you notice that?" She moved to stand in front of Bartlett, the two of them positioned sideways in front of the closet. "I hope you don't think I'm too forward."

Bartlett cleared his throat. "Not at all."

She slid her hands around his neck. "I'm very glad to hear it."

From his vantage point, Winston could see her fiddling with the ring, obviously judging when to dose him. Winston was certain that the drug was intended to make Bartlett pliable enough to reveal the laptop's password. But that type of maneuver was always dicey. Give too much, and your subject could pass out before revealing any information. Give too little, and they wouldn't be susceptible.

And there was the small matter that the computer wasn't in plain sight.

"You must be doing more relaxing than working," she said. "I assumed an accountant would be surrounded by papers. At the very least, I would have thought you'd have a computer."

"It's in the room safe. I trust hotels, but not maids." He stood up. "Besides, who wants work around us while we're sharing some wine and what? Oysters? Dessert?"

"Either sounds wonderful." She was practically purring, and Winston wasn't sure who he wanted to strangle more—her or the accountant.

He leaned forward as if to kiss her, but she pulled back, then pressed her fingertip over his lips. "I like anticipation," she whispered, and it took all of Winston's strength to keep himself from bursting out of the closet and confronting her right then.

How many collective hours had he spent in a sensual haze, his cock hard as steel, his body hot with need. "I love feeling like this," she'd tell him. "Needy and desperate. The buildup of anticipation. Don't you?"

God, yes, he'd loved it. So much that it became a sensual game for the both of them. Out in public, on the couch watching television. Any time one or the other had the urge, they'd start an hours-long sensual dance that would end with a wild, explosive taking, all the more potent because they had held back for so long.

It had been intimate and intense. And, he'd believed, only for them.

"Anticipation is good," Bartlett whispered.

"I'm very glad to hear it."

"Why don't you get comfortable? There's a robe on the back of the bathroom door."

"Is there?" She glanced over her shoulder, her brow furrowed slightly. Winston was certain she was weighing her options, an assumption that was proved when she said, "But if I go in there, you might forget all about me."

"I won't think about anything but you, and how I'm going to make you feel for the rest of the evening." He grinned, all smug and confident. "Anticipation, right?"

She turned back to him. "You are a fast learner," she purred, and though Winston hated himself for it, he felt the cold fingers of jealousy crawl up his spine.

As Winston watched, Bartlett nodded toward the bathroom. "Go on. I'll order."

She hesitated, and Winston was certain he knew what she was thinking. If he were in her position, he'd be weighing the same options. Was it better to play this out or to show her hand now?

As he would have done, she headed toward the bathroom. Until she actually accessed the safe and saw the laptop, she couldn't rely on what Bartlett had told her. Better to keep her cover until she had full certainty that the mission could be completed.

And that, of course, was why he was still standing behind the louvered door, watching the drama play out in front of him.

He heard the click of the bathroom door and watched as Bartlett loosened his tie. The man had been a little shy and awkward in the bar, but in this room he was full of confidence. The prick.

Now, he walked to the closet. Winston tensed, then stepped to the side as one half of the door slid open. Bartlett took a step forward, and Winston moved fast, grabbing the accountant's arm, flipping him around, and trapping him against the metal frame in which the closet doors slid open.

"Wh—"

Winston clapped his arm over the man's mouth, then whispered. "Quiet. I'm not going to hurt you. I have a gun, but I'm not using it. I'm here to help you. The woman you're with—she's not what you think. She's a professional assassin, and Hawthorne sent her to kill you."

That got through to the man. Bartlett's eyes widened, then cut sideways as if he was trying to look to the bathroom.

"Quiet," Winston repeated as he loosened his hand over the other man's mouth. "I'm here to help. I'll take care of the woman. Then I'll get you and the laptop somewhere safe."

"Safe?"

"Where you'll be protected until you can testify. I'm working with the SOC. Seagrave sent me."

The man visibly paled. "Oh, God."

"I know. We need to get you where Hawthorne and his people can't find you. Just do as I say and I'll make sure this goes smoothly."

Bartlett nodded, his eyes wide with fear.

Cautiously, Winston loosened his hand. At the same time, he heard the click of the bathroom door. Winston pushed Bartlett all the way into the closet, then shoved past him into the room as he drew his weapon.

"There wasn't a robe," Linda called as an electronic beep sounded from inside the closet. There was a teasing lilt to her voice as she added, "So I just borrowed a towel."

Winston silently cursed Bartlett for getting into the safe before he had Linda contained, but he couldn't deal with the man right then. Not now that Linda had come into sight.

He saw her mouth open in shock, then felt the hard bash of metal crashing against the back of his skull. He fell forward as the hotel iron dropped to the carpet next to him. He rolled to his side, swinging his arm wide so as to knock Bartlett's legs out from under him even while Winston brought the gun around to lock onto Linda.

She froze, her mouth open, her eyes as wide as if she'd just seen a ghost.

At the same time, Bartlett's laptop went flying, landing hard on the thick carpet as Bartlett managed to keep his balance. Winston cursed, but kept the gun on Linda.

"Why the fuck did you bean me?" he snapped at the accountant. "I'm here to help you."

He expected Bartlett to snatch up the laptop, then go cower in a corner. Instead, the accountant bolted for the door, terror coming off him like waves.

What the hell?

Winston clambered to his feet and followed, keeping the gun trained on Linda even as he paused in the doorway, weighing his options as Bartlett plowed through the stairwell door. They were only on the third floor, which meant he'd be at the lobby before Winston could call down for security to apprehend him. If he followed, Linda would bolt.

Plus, the laptop was still in the room. Two birds in the hand and one on the fly.

Not perfect—not by a long shot—but he was staying. And it had taken him maybe half a second to run through his various options.

Now decided, he shut the door and held the gun steady, aimed directly at her heart.

"Winston." Her voice was steady. Flat. Without a hint of remorse. Hell, without a hint of anything. "Would it be cliché if I said that this is quite the surprise?"

He shook his head slowly, wishing he could unhear her flat, cold words. "You think I won't pull the trigger? You think I wouldn't gladly destroy you? You ruined my life, damn you. You killed the woman I loved."

One brow rose, and she released her hold on the towel. It fell to her feet, leaving her naked in front of him, and just as beautiful as he remembered. "Maybe I did," she said, taking a single step forward. "And if it's payback you want, now's the time."

CHAPTER SIX

Almost six years before...

The single towel is barely enough to cover me, but I hold the edges together with one hand between my breasts as I meet his eyes. Not two seconds ago I'd stepped out of my bathroom, still damp from the shower, because I'd left my new deodorant and toothbrush in the grocery bag on the coffee table. What I found instead was Sheriff Winston Starr.

I keep my chin up, determined not to be flustered even though my heart is beating like a butterfly's wings, and not just because he's so damn good-looking with that muscular body, rugged face, and kind eyes that crinkle when he smiles.

No, the bigger reason for my nerves is that I have secrets. And if this small town sheriff has found them out ... well, my bosses aren't going to like that.

I clear my throat, realizing that neither one of us has spoken. "Do you want to tell me what you're doing in my apartment?"

He takes off his hat as he glances down at the floor. When he lifts his head, the apology is right there in his eyes. "Linda, I'm sorry." He gestures behind him. "I knocked. The door swung open."

"Oh." *Dammit.* I draw a breath and offer him a small smile. "I've called the landlord twice. I should have just fixed it myself, but I haven't had the time." I shrug. "New job. New town." *Busy secret life...*

"I can take care of that for you."

"Oh." The flutter in my chest starts up again, underscored by a nice, warm glow. "You don't have to do that."

"I want to." He slides his hands into the pockets of his light brown slacks that pair with the uniform shirt, decorated with his badge and other symbols of his office.

"Well, I won't turn down the help. Thanks." When he returns my smile, I feel lit from within. Light and fresh and new. I realize I'm smiling like an idiot. I always seem to be smiling around this man. An unexpected reality that makes my job both easier and harder.

I've only been in town for two weeks. I lived

here for a year in high school when my dad was dragging me all over the country as he scrambled to find work. He'd died here, too, when there'd been a blowout at the rig. I'd stayed at a friend's house for the rest of the year, then moved to Wisconsin when my aunt came to claim me.

I ran away six months after that, got my GED, made my own way.

But now here I am back again. The fact that my daddy had died in that blowout helped me land the job in the mayor's office. That, and the fact that my real bosses pulled a few strings behind the scenes.

My cover job is easy enough. Mostly I file, answer the phones, and fetch coffee for the folks higher up the ladder, which includes pretty much everyone.

I'd been carrying a tray with four coffees from the cafeteria back to the mayor's chambers when I saw Winston for the first time just four short days ago. Hades is small enough that the city and county offices share a building, and he was walking into the cafeteria as I was walking out.

He'd taken the tray from me without a word, then fallen in step beside me. Any other man, and I would have icily berated him for being a conde-scending, presumptuous prick. With Winston, I floated along as we made small talk that didn't seem small at all.

When we paused outside the mayor's office, he said, "I'm glad I was right."

I frowned. "About what?"

"You know," he said, then gave me back my tray before tapping the brim of his hat and walking away.

I watched him go, my pulse beating in my throat. *Yeah. I knew.*

For the next few days, our eyes would meet whenever we crossed paths. Once, he walked me to my car, and when our hands brushed casually, I felt the shock of it so intensely that I'd actually gasped out loud, my skin burning from a full-body blush. And I'm not a woman who blushes.

But we haven't really talked yet. Haven't shared a meal. Hell, we haven't even shared coffee. And yet here he is in my living room, and as much as I want to fight my own reaction, it feels as if he belongs here.

There's a pull between us. Something physicists might never understand but which nonetheless exists. The kind of chemical reaction that had me coming home after work and stripping off my clothes, then sliding into bed and foregoing dinner for the pleasure of my fantasies. The kind of obsession that had my mind wandering during my pre-dawn meetings when, honestly, I should have been paying more attention.

Now, standing in front of me in my living room,

he clears his throat. "I know I shouldn't have come in. But with the door open like that..."

"You thought I had an intruder?"

The corner of his mouth lifts in a slow grin. "Crossed my mind. Hades might be a safe little town, but you still need to be careful."

I almost laugh. In a lot of ways, he's an innocent. Especially about this town. He sees only the cute little houses and the charming Main Street. As far as he's concerned, the only problems are a few drunk and disorderlies or teenagers stealing candy and DVDs. He might be the sheriff, but Hades' rot is so deep he doesn't even see it.

One day, though, it will bubble to the top. There'll be an assault case or a body discovered far out in the county. He'll get sucked in. Start looking. And once he opens his eyes, he'll see me standing right in front of him.

That reality wrenches at my heart, especially since I know what I need to do now. I should thank him for checking the door, then ask him to leave. But I don't. Instead, I say, "There's no intruder here. Nobody but you."

He chuckles, obviously hearing the flirtatious tone in my voice. Then he takes another step closer. "I should have left," he says, "but I heard the shower. So I stayed."

"Oh." I lick my lips, feeling young and innocent. I'm twenty-five, and haven't felt young since my mother walked out. I was five then. And I'm damn sure not innocent. "Why?"

His head tilts to the side, his eyes never leaving mine, and I feel the heat of his gaze all the way down to my bare toes. "You know," he says, and my nipples harden and my sex throbs with longing.

My breath catches in my throat as he takes one more step forward.

"This isn't normal." My voice sounds far away.

"No," he says, "it's not. Nothing's been normal since the first moment I saw you." He meets my eyes, and I see a future there, the kind of future I never thought I could have. That I never will. It's like looking into pain, because I know how this will end.

And yet I can't look away.

"Do you want me to go?"

"No." I meet his eyes, then drop the towel. "I want you to stay."

CHAPTER SEVEN

"Winston?" I say now, as the memory of our shared past cuts through me, cold and bittersweet. "Is it really you?"

I take a step toward him, wanting desperately to touch him. But another more rational part wishes that he weren't here at all. "What are you doing here?"

"Just stop right there," he orders as I start to take a second step.

I freeze. There was a time when I'd known without a shadow of a doubt that he would never hurt me. That he'd die to protect me. But that time is definitely not now.

His hand on the gun is firm, and the barrel doesn't shake at all. If I've rattled him, he's not showing it. And there's no doubt in my mind that he'll pull that trigger if I don't do exactly what he says.

It's no less than I deserve, but that simple truth saddens me. I never thought this day would come, and now that it has, all I want to do is run away. But not from the gun. No, what I want is to escape that hard, lost look in his eyes.

"We should talk." I cock my head toward the bed. "Can I sit?"

His eyes narrow as he looks me up and down. It's a cold, assessing look. Nothing remotely sensual about it, and yet my traitorous body responds. My skin heats. My nipples tighten. My skin flushes.

I remember with sudden clarity the last time we'd been together. The living room had been lit with firelight, and we'd drunk wine and made love on a blanket spread across our living room floor. I cherish the memory, and a knife-edge of anger cuts through me because I know that the same memory only hurts him now.

"Please," I say, edging sideways.

"Don't fucking move."

I freeze. "Why are you here?" I ask again. "And why do you have a gun? I thought you left police work."

"You thought?" he repeats. "You *thought*?" He takes a step toward me, but not too close. "Funny. I didn't think the dead could think."

"Winston—"

"*No.*" The word is sharp and cold as steel, and I see the pain reflected all over his face. Pain that I caused. "Tell me."

I lick my lips. "I know that you left Hades. You moved to California. You quit law enforcement and retired and volunteered at an animal shelter."

I'd been glad of that. That the life insurance I'd put in place had allowed him to leave police work behind. And he'd finally been able to get a dog. I'd told him I was allergic back in the day, but it wasn't true. In reality, my handlers didn't want any creature in my life that might, literally, be able to sniff out my secrets.

His eyes narrow slightly as he studies my face. "Is that supposed to make me feel better? That you kept an eye on me? Tell me what you saw, Linda. Because if it wasn't a man broken completely in two, then you had the wrong damn picture."

"I know," I say. "I wasn't—I mean, I didn't—"

"*What?*"

"I wasn't spying on you. I only wanted to know that you'd be okay."

He laughs at that. A hard, raucous sound. "Okay? *Okay?* Are you insane? My wife was dead —at least I thought she was. I'd been ripped to pieces. And you've been keeping tabs on me for all these years?"

"No. I—"

"What?" he snaps, and I have to work not to recoil from the vitriol in his tone.

"I stopped watching. Once you were settled in Orange County with your house and your work at the shelter, I never paid attention again." I lift my chin. "It hurt too much to watch what you were doing and not say anything."

"I'm supposed to believe that?"

"It's the truth. Every day since that horrible day in Hades, I've tried to get you out of my head." I lick my lips, knowing I'm revealing too much, but dammit, he deserves to know. Or maybe I just want to soothe a little bit of my own guilt. "Every day, I've failed."

"If you're looking for sympathy, you're looking in the wrong place."

"I know." I run my sweaty palms over my bare hips then look down at the carpeting.

The truth is, I betrayed him. I hurt him. And if I could heal those wounds, I would. It was necessary, but that doesn't make the pain any less. And though my heart ached for what we couldn't have, I know that the pain he suffered cut so much deeper.

I can't tell him that, though. Not the truth of it. But even if I could, what would it matter? We can never get back what we lost. Hell, we were never supposed to have it in the first place. We were always living on borrowed time. I'm just the only one of the two of us who knew it.

That cold reality has haunted me for years. I used to believe the pain couldn't get worse, but now I know that I'd been a fool. I'm alive, after all. Before tonight, he'd loved a memory.

But now...

Well, now I've left him with nothing at all. Nothing except a deep void to be filled with hate and regret and sorrow.

I let the pain and the memories wash over me, then lift my head and focus again on that gun. "Why are you here?" I force my voice to break, wanting to sound scared. Desperate. Honestly, it's not that hard. "Did you track me down? Is that why you have a gun? Did you go back to police work? Did you come here to—to hurt me?"

For a moment, his eyes are hard. The he scoffs and shakes his head. "I'm not a cop, but I still carry. You've seen what I've seen—all the crime, your wife murdered—well, carrying a gun doesn't seem like overkill."

"No pun intended?" I tease, trying for a light tone.

I must succeed at least a little, because I see his mouth twitch.

"Did you come here looking for me?"

He looks me right in the eyes. "I've thought you were dead for years. I saw you, and I was shocked. It couldn't be you. How could my dead wife be alive? But there you were, just sitting there in the hotel bar."

"A coincidence." The word brushes softly over my lips, so sweet I can almost taste it. *He didn't know. He didn't come here to find me.* "You just happened to be in town?"

He shrugs. "On business."

"Which is?"

"Would you believe I consult on movies?"

"Really?"

He shrugs again, looking a little embarrassed. "Small town sheriff. Lots of TV shows and movies want to make it seem real."

I nod, relieved he's only living the Hollywood version of law enforcement. "Must be fun."

"I think we just hit the limit on small talk."

"Right." I manage a smile. "So you saw me in the bar, then followed us up to the room. The Winston I knew before would have waltzed over to our table and had it out with me."

"I'm not the man you knew before." There's something hollow in his voice when he says that. Something that makes me very, very sad.

I swallow. "No, I suppose you're not."

He shoves his free hand into his pocket, his eyes looking everywhere before finally settling on me. "When I first saw you, just sitting there with the asshole who bolted, I was sure it couldn't be you. You're dead, right? My wife's been dead for years.

But I followed, anyway. My gut knew what my mind didn't want to admit. And when I knocked on the door and the asshole told me your name was — well. That was a dead giveaway, wasn't it?"

"No pun intended?" I say, hoping for another hint of laughter from this overused joke. But there's no reaction this time. None at all. Instead, he just stares me down.

"Michelle Moon," he says. "That asshole you came here to fuck said your name was Michelle Moon."

He says the name like it's a betrayal. Which, of course, he thinks it is. *You're the moon to my Starr,"* he used to tease me. And as for Michelle...

"I'm truly sorry about that." The words come out in a whisper. "When you heard it, you must have thought—"

"I didn't think," he snaps. "I didn't have to. The situation was clear enough. You were alive. You'd betrayed me."

I lick my lips. "So you just knocked on the door and my date volunteered my name?"

He nods. "I said I was an old friend of Linda Starr's. He told me I had the wrong room. That your name was Michelle Moon."

I press my lips together.

"I asked to talk to you," Winston continues, "and he said you were in the bathroom." He shrugs. "I don't know what came over me, but I pushed my way in. And once I was past the door I told him we used to be married. That shocked him but I said that I only wanted to talk to you."

"What did he say?"

"Offered me a chair."

I cock my head to one side. "Really? And then after this polite interchange, he slammed you in the head with an iron?"

"He blindsided me," Winston says. "Considering I pulled my gun when I heard the bathroom door open, I can't blame the guy too much. At least he was chivalrous enough to try to save you." He looks at me hard. "Then again, he's the one who bolted and left you with the crazy man waving a gun. To my way of thinking, that makes your boyfriend a real dick."

"He's not my boyfriend." Under the circumstances, it hardly matters, but I want him to know that. Not that it can make up for anything.

"So it was just a pick up? A quick fuck? Well, that makes me feel better."

"It should," I say. I wave a hand to indicate my still-naked body. "You've stripped me of all pretense, Winston. You want the truth? The truth is that I haven't been with anyone since you. Not seriously. But sometimes, especially when I'm on the road..."

"You don't live here, either?"

"I came in for a conference. I'm an office manager in a plumbing supply company in Tulsa."

"Sounds thrilling."

"It's not."

"So the chivalrous guy who bolted and left you with the potentially crazed ex-husband, he was just a hook-up?"

"I'll be leaving a few choice comments on his profile later." I'm trying for levity, but when he doesn't react, I try another tact. "I've been so lonely." I watch his face, hoping that he can hear the truth in my voice.

"Then I guess you made a mistake pretending to die."

I feel the tears well, and I don't try to hold them. "No," I whisper. "That was horrible and it hurt both of us, but it wasn't a mistake."

"What the hell are you talking about?"

"I never wanted to leave you."

"You expect me to believe that?"

I glance away, not quite able to meet his eyes. "I don't think I have the right to expect anything from you anymore."

My palms are sweaty again, and I take a sideways step towards the bed, intending to grab the spread, but he gives his head one quick sideways shake, the gun still trained on me. "Stay put."

I freeze. I don't think he'd really shoot me, but all things considered I wouldn't be surprised.

"Go on. You were telling me you didn't want to leave." There's a harsh tone to his voice, as if he doesn't believe me. Well, why would he?

"It's the truth." It really is. I would have done anything to stay with him, but anything wasn't possible. So instead I did everything I could to protect him. "I knew you were working on a case, remember? Something big. Something scary. But that's all you told me. Corruption in the local government, you said. And I knew there'd been a murder. But you never gave me the details."

Winston nods. "I remember."

"Well, that's it, really. I knew something was going on, and I knew it was bad. And then one night when you were out, someone came to the house."

"Who?"

"I don't know." I glance toward the bed. "Please. Can I at least sit?"

He hesitates, then nods. I move to the bed, then sit on the edge, my legs tight together. I reach for a pillow to pull into my lap, but he shakes his head.

I draw in a breath, and cross my hand over my breasts. I'm not modest—in my business, it's really not an asset—but right now I feel genuinely exposed.

For a moment, I think he's going to tell me to put my hands at my sides. When he doesn't, I relax a little, then have to remind myself to be vigilant. I still don't know what the situation is. He says it's a coincidence, but is it really? He could be telling the truth, but he could just as easily be lying.

That's another reality of the world I live in now —everybody lies, and there's not one goddamn person I truly trust. Winston was the last, and now I can't even trust him.

"What?"

I force myself not to cringe, realizing my uncertainty must have shown on my face. I'm getting sloppy. Or, rather, Winston is making me sloppy.

"I was just remembering that night," I lie.

"When someone came to the house." His tone is harsh, as if he doesn't believe me. Smart man. But in this case it's true. Just not the entire truth.

"He said he worked with the local police," I continue. "That there were things going down, and that you were in the middle of them, and that if you kept poking around you would end up dead."

"Go on."

"He told me that the only way that you would survive this was if you pulled your nose out of the entire mess, but that you were like a dog with a bone. And you wouldn't give up unless something huge distracted you." I meet his eyes, and feel real tears prick at my own. "He said the only thing big enough to distract you was me. He said I had to die."

"And you were such a little martyr that you died for me."

"I don't blame you for not believing me, but it's true." I watch him, trying to read his expression. It's blank at first, and then I see the shift on his face. The shadow in his eyes. The hint of a frown at the corners of his mouth. I think that he understands. That, maybe just a little, he's beginning to trust me. Most of all, that he believes me.

I know it's a risk, but I stand, then take a step toward him. I see his body stiffen, but he doesn't step back, and so I move forward another few inches, then another. He's still holding the gun, but I reach for his other hand, and take it in my own.

If this were a movie, the room would be filled with starbursts. His touch is so familiar, so wonderful. I've missed it. And oh, dear God, I want more. It's not just the feel of his hand in mine that affects me. It's the connection, and it ricochets through me, making my body react in ways that I wish it wouldn't, because it reveals too damn much. Especially since I'm standing there naked in front of him.

But this isn't about sex or attraction. I need him to believe me. And while I don't like being vulnerable, not even in front of Winston, at least he can see the truth of it on my body. "I've missed you so much," I whisper. "So, so much."

He pulls his hand free, then steps back. "And yet you stayed away."

"I had to. They said if you ever learned the truth, they'd kill you." There's a harshness in my voice that I wish wasn't there. But it's the truth, damn it, at least mostly. And it's probably the only truly selfless thing I've ever done. I want him to know it. I want him to know that even though I did betray him, I only did it to save his life.

"Are you remarried?" I blurt the question out without thinking. "Seeing anybody?"

"No." The word is hard. Firm. The answer makes me sad that he's alone, but mostly it makes me happy. I know it shouldn't. This is ending tonight. I'm going to extricate myself from this mess come hell or high water. I'll curse the bad luck of running into my husband and I'll move on.

I haven't lied about the danger to him. Odds are Billy Hawthorne's people are watching me. And if they think that I actually arranged to contact Hades' former sheriff, well I could very well be a dead woman.

Right now, I'm probably safe, but the longer I'm with him, the more the danger increases.

The truth is, I won't see him after tonight and it's a miracle that we crossed paths at all. I've never been one for signs, but I'm a wiz with justifications. And at this particular moment there's nothing else for me to do except extricate myself from this mess, then wait and regroup. I'll find Bartlett again easily enough. And the laptop's still in this room.

I take another step toward Winston, who holds his ground. We're only inches apart now. I haven't done anything this impulsive or foolish in years. Not since I was with this man, back when there was joy in my life. Back when he was the joy in my life.

"Don't," he says as I lift my hand and put it on his hip. The muscles in his face are tight, his voice harsher than I've ever heard it.

"Please," I say. I step back, then press my palm between my breasts and slowly slide my own hand down over my belly, then let my fingers curl between my legs as I bite my lip to fight off a moan of pleasure.

"Christ, Linda."

I watch his face, desperate for him to touch me. Not because this is a ploy to get me out of this mess —or at least, not entirely—but because I've been numb since the night I supposedly died. *No.* I *did* die. In every way that matters.

No, I want his hands on me so that I'll feel alive again, even if only for a little while.

"Please," I repeat. "Hate me if you want, but touch me now."

For a moment he does nothing. Then he holsters his gun. I watch, then raise my eyes to his. "Don't even think about it."

I laugh. "Guns aren't really my thing. You know that."

He makes a scoffing sound, then reaches for my upper arm, pulling me toward him. "Take off the damn ring," he says, lifting my hand.

The mention of the ring brings me up short. One prick, and he'd be totally amenable to anything I wanted, unless of course he got too much of a dose and passed out. But neither of those situations sound appealing to me. It's not what I want. I want the man. I want to steal back a remnant of our past to keep with me when I get out of this mess and walk out that door.

Still, the mention of the ring disturbs me, and I look at him curiously. "What's wrong with my ring?"

"That setting'll scrape the hell out of me." His hand slides down to my fingers and he tugs it off. I hold my breath, afraid he'll discover its secrets. "If I'm getting scratched, it'll be with teeth or nails."

He releases me and backs away, then leaves me long enough to set the ring on the dresser by the television, along with his holster and weapon. Relief washes over me. If he's putting away his gun, then he trusts me.

He turns, and for a moment he simply stands there. Then he lets his eyes roam slowly over me as sparks ignite inside me. "I should hate you," he says, as he comes closer, then closes his hands over my shoulders.

"I know."

His hands glide down to cup my breasts, and I gasp. "I should," he says. "Hell, maybe I do. But it doesn't matter. Right now, I just want you."

"Yes," I murmur as I arch back, losing myself in the feel of his hands on my skin.

He eases me sideways so that we fall in a tumble onto the bed. I'm on my back, his hands moving as if he needs to feel every inch of me to be certain that I'm real.

When he shifts to straddle me, I moan. He's still dressed, and I'm naked, my body so responsive. I've missed this. Missed him. And even though I know this isn't real—even though I know that I'm only playing this role to get out of this situation—I still want this moment. I want his touch. I want him inside me.

I reach for his belt and fumble for the buckle. He finishes the work, then slides the belt off and tosses it on the bed as I work on the button and zipper.

He bends forward, his hands sliding up to my breasts again, his fingers pinching my nipples. I'm naked and he's clothed, and the rough feel of the material of his slacks against my naked flesh is wildly enticing.

He lifts my arms above my head, then bends to

kiss me. I close my eyes, losing myself in the heat of the moment as his hand roams down my side, the curve of my waist, the swell of my hip. For a moment, I feel no contact, then his large hand tightens around my wrists.

I open my eyes and try to yank my arms down, but he's straddling my ribcage now, his knees digging painfully into my sides.

"Winston!" I cry out his name, but it's myself that I'm cursing. Because not only has he trapped me under his weight, he's bound my wrists to the ornate ironwork of the bedframe with his belt.

"You son of a bitch." I jerk against the bond, only to wince when the unyielding leather cuts into my tender skin.

Winston leans back, his eyes going cold as he looks at me, still straddling me. He cups my breasts as he leans forward, looking straight into my eyes. "And now, my lovely wife, I think it's time we had a real conversation."

CHAPTER EIGHT

"G oddammit, Winston, let me up."

"Sure thing. I'll get right on that."

There's sarcasm in his voice, but when he comes and stands right by me and starts to fiddle with the belt, I think maybe he really is going to free me. Then I hear the distinctive *zzzzzp* and realize that, no. All he's done is tie me down even tighter with cable ties.

He steps back, the belt now in his hand. "There you go."

"You bastard."

He grins. "Pretty much."

I make a frustrated growling noise as I tug against the headboard, but to no effect. All I manage to do is make my wrists sore. But what the hell, right? I deserve the pain. I completely misjudged the situation, and all because being around this man has thrown me completely off my game.

I yank at the bonds again. "Let me go, damn you. What do you think you're doing?"

"You should have done your homework better, sugar. You should have been more interested in what became of the man who was your husband."

"*Is* my husband," I say. "I'm alive, aren't I?"

I see the comprehension on his face as he realizes the impact of my still walking this earth. But he doesn't smile. There's absolutely no hint on his gorgeous, rugged face, that still being tied to me could possibly be a good thing.

Fuck.

"I'm not too sure about that," he says. "I don't think you are my Linda anymore. After all, Linda Starr is legally dead. I know, because I'm the one they handed the death certificate to."

My heart twists painfully in my chest. "Winston, I—"

"Doesn't much matter, though, does it?" His eyes narrow from where he stands above me beside the bed. "After all, you're not my Linda. You're Michelle Moon, and God knows, I've never met her."

I turn my head, not wanting to meet his eyes. I'm still naked, but I haven't really felt exposed until this moment.

"People pick new names all the time," I say.

"And I told you the truth. I had to get a new life in order to keep you safe."

"Well, sugar, I surely do appreciate you looking out for me all these years. It warms a man's heart."

If it weren't so tragic, I'd be laughing. Winston used to thicken his Texas drawl just because it amused me. It's not amusing me now. I closed my eyes for a moment, gathering my thoughts. When I'm ready, I open them and look back at him.

He's seated beside me. His hip resting against my thigh, his hand on the other side of me. It's close and intimate, and I feel far too exposed and vulnerable. It's not a feeling I like. I'm certain he knows that, and I force myself to keep a steady gaze as I look into his eyes and say, "For better or for worse, remember? However it plays out, I'm still your wife."

"It seems to me, couples break up all the time. I think that even if a judge needed a reason to make it official, I've got one."

I turned my head to the side. He'd always been sentimental, and I thought that he would still have some compassion for me. Some nugget I could mine in order to convince him to untie me. Apparently it's not going to be as easy as I'd hoped.

Once again, I draw a breath and look at him. "All right, then, you tell me. You say I should have gotten to know you better? Why don't you introduce me to the man who is my husband?"

"Well, that's a pretty long story, darlin'. It's true that I'm not with the Sheriff's Department anymore. But I do still know things. Hell, I even know a few things about you."

I keep my expression perfectly composed. "Is that a fact? What kinds of things do you know? Other than how to tie a woman down. Should I be worried about my virtue at this point? Is it rape if you're still my husband?"

"Don't worry," he says, his eyes cold. "I'm not going to touch you."

They shouldn't, but both his words and his tone rattle me. And in that moment, I have to acknowledge my disappointment. I'd played a sensual game as a means to an end, but I can't deny that I'd wanted his touch. Once upon a time, this man had been my heart and soul. And even when I'd been mired in a shit storm of secrets and lies, I could always find comfort in his arms. His kisses soothing me. His touch reassuring me.

He hadn't known my secrets, but he had always known my heart, and the fact that I can no longer claim that comfort from him bothers me even more than the fact that he turned the tables on me, leaving me tied down and frustrated.

With a Herculean effort, I gather my thoughts, telling myself I need to at least pretend to be the professional agent I'm trained to be. "All right," I say slowly. "I'll bite. What kind of things do you think you know?"

He flashes a sideways grin. "You tell me."

I roll my eyes. "That's not the way it works. You say you have information about me? Prove it."

"Well," he says drawing the word out in a perfect West Texas drawl. "I suppose I could do that. Or maybe I should use this to convince you to talk." As he speaks, he gets up and moves to the dresser. He turns around, holding that hideously ugly ring, and I have to force myself not to wince. Apparently, he does know what secret is hidden inside.

I meet his eyes. "Then use it."

"At least you're not denying it. But I won't. I imagine you're trained to withstand Sodium Pentothal or whatever you have in here." He puts the ring on the bedside table. "You keep it. Use it to seduce your marks. Although, honestly, with your skills in the bedroom, I'm surprised you need to use a drug. How lucky am I to have been able to witness those unique talents up close and personal?"

"I never faked a thing with you," I snap. The words are true enough, but I've said them mostly to cover the wild spinning of my thoughts as I shift the puzzle pieces in my mind to fit this new reality. "And in case it escaped your notice, you're the one who tied me up. Naked, I might add. Not exactly what nice little boys do."

What does he know? What exactly does he know?

"Oh, come on, Linda. Please." He looks at me with so much disgust I actually turn my head away. "You're trying to make me look like the villain of this piece? How exactly does that work when you're the one who faked her death and now earns her keep as a killer for hire?"

My entire body goes cold, but I hold his gaze. "I don't know what you're talking about."

"Yes," he says. "You do."

I say nothing for a moment, weighing my options. And the sad truth is I don't have many. Many? Try none. So I don't argue. I don't protest. I don't deny. I just turn my face away from him and say, very simply, "Put a blanket over me."

I want to cry. I never wanted him to know that truth. But, dammit, I'm too well trained. And though I close my eyes, the tears won't come. I can't even fake them and hope for his sympathy.

To his credit, he doesn't flout his victory. Instead, he puts the blanket over me, just as I'd asked.

I swallow, then murmur, "Thank you."

"Tell me about Hades."

I fight the impulse to open my eyes and turn to

look at him. His voice is further away now as if he's standing across the room.

"Tell me the truth this time," he says.

I stay silent.

"Damn it, Linda, Michelle, whatever the fuck your name is, I deserve the truth. What the hell, right? It's not like I can use it against you."

That confuses me enough that I do turn my head and look at him. He's grinning, looking straight at me with an expression so cold and dangerous I feel even more exposed despite the blanket.

"Spousal privilege, darlin'. Like you said—we're still married."

"If I believed there was even a kernel of anything real left between us," I say, "I'd tell you everything."

"And if I believed there was ever anything real between us, I'd untie you." He stares down at me. "Talk."

I stay silent.

He draws an exasperated breath. "As far as the world knows, you're dead. Which from my perspective, means that you can leave this room as you are or as the public records think you are."

"You wouldn't kill me."

"Wouldn't I?"

"You forget how well I know you."

"*Knew* me," he says. "You don't have a clue who I am now."

He's right about that. Maybe he consults for Hollywood, and maybe he doesn't, but the man who tied me to this bed and knows that I'm an assassin is neither naive nor uninformed. I don't know how deep his clearance goes, but I'd lay odds he's in intelligence. Probably got pulled in after my purported death. He'd have wanted answers, after all.

As for the threat, though ... well, about that, he's bluffing. I'm almost certain of it.

Too bad *almost* could get me killed. And while sometimes I think that dying would be easier than living the life I'm stuck with, I'm not ready to leave this earth.

"I'm waiting," he says. "And we both know you owe me the truth."

CHAPTER NINE

W inston wanted to hate her. That longing —that need—sat in his gut like a stone.

He wished he could erase her from his mind, the pain he'd felt after she died and the joy he'd known during their time together. Yes, even that. He wanted it gone. Wiped out of existence.

Because what she was now stripped it of all meaning. An assassin. A fucking assassin. It was surreal, and the sooner he could hand her off to an SOC agent and then bring Bartlett and the laptop in safe, the better.

And he'd do that soon—he would.

But first he wanted to know the truth. No, he *needed* to know it. And he was happy to keep her strapped down on this bed for as long as it took to get the story out of her lying, betraying little mouth.

"Talk," he said, but she only met his gaze,

looking back with an intensity that matched his own. Her boldness infuriated him.

Even so, damn him, he couldn't help but notice how lovely she was. She'd always had a glow about her, a vibrancy. Making love to her had been like losing himself in a lightning bolt. Wild and stunning and shocking and beautiful, and often times so very unexpected.

The irony wasn't lost on him. He'd liked that about her—the surprises she gave him in bed and in their marriage. But he'd never seen this biggest surprise of all coming.

"Talk," he repeated, his voice tight. "And in case you're even the slightest bit unclear on the point, keep in mind that you're talking for your life. Bullshit me, and you'll be dead all over again, only this time it will be for real."

She said nothing.

A blinding wave of fury cut through him, and he crossed to the dresser in three long strides and grabbed his gun. He was back at her side in seconds, the muzzle pressed against her temple.

"You won't hurt me."

He held her gaze for a full three seconds. It felt like forever. But he saw the way she shrank into herself. For a moment, just a moment, he hated the hardness within him that made him say the words. But he said them anyway. "Yes. I will. Now talk."

She closed her eyes, but whether to gather her

thoughts or to block him from her vision, he didn't know. He almost thought he was going to have to prod her again, but then she began to speak, her eyes still closed.

"I was in college—really struggling to pay rent and tuition—and a friend dragged me to one of those career fairs on a lark. The NSC and the CIA were there, along with all the branches of the military and the FBI too, everybody offering a chance at a paid higher education, exciting opportunity, yada, yada. No one knows how to sell like the government does."

She shifted on the bed, wincing a bit as the cable ties bit into the flesh of her wrists. He expected her to beg for release again and had to admit that he was impressed when she didn't.

"Go on."

"I thought being an agent would be the height of coolness. I told you about my childhood. None of that was a lie. My mom died when I was young, my dad in an explosion. And the aunt who was supposed to raise me was useless, so I bolted. I pretty much grew up on the streets. Had to make my own way. It was not what I'd call an ideal life."

He nodded, remembering the one conversation they'd had in which she talked about her past. They'd made love afterwards slowly and sweetly, and before they'd fallen asleep, she turned to him and whispered one thing. "Please," she'd said. "I don't ever want to talk about that again."

He'd honored that wish, and he was struck now by the fact that she was bringing it up again. He was making her bring it up again. Despite himself, he said, "I'm sorry. I didn't want to dredge that up."

The corner of her mouth turned up in the smallest of smiles. "Thank you for that," she shifted on the bed and started over again. "It's not even that relevant, but I think that my background made me a good candidate for deep cover work, because I came up through the ranks pretty quickly."

"Did you?"

She must have noticed the edge in his voice, because she smiled a bit before answering. "I enjoyed the work. And I sailed through training. I was like a prodigy. All modesty aside, I really was good at my job."

He thought about the efficiency with which she'd killed the man on the roof, and he crossed his arms over his chest. "Oh, I believe you."

Something in his tone must have made her ill at ease, because she stumbled for a bit before catching her rhythm again. "At any rate, I went through training quickly, and about a year before I met you, I was made a full-time agent. Believe me, you can learn a lot in a year in a place like that. I traveled the world. Saw exciting and exotic locations, and had my life put in danger more times than I'd like to count."

"Well, look at you. Might as well be your own movie star. Must've been disappointing to end up assigned to marry the likes of me."

"That was no assignment," she snapped, the fury in her voice seeming real enough that it made him take a step back. He looked at her face to find her looking right back at him, her eyes filled with both anger and sadness. Maybe even regret. "Please tell me you don't really believe that."

"I don't know what to believe," he said. "I really don't."

"Me," she said. "Maybe you should just believe me."

He wanted to laugh. "Because you've given me so much cause for trust."

She drew in a breath. "I don't blame you for that, but you need to know that I always loved you. That was never an act. Never part of my training."

He forced his face to stay expressionless as he leaned back in the chair, his feet extended out in front of him. "Wouldn't that be nice to believe?"

"Believe what you want, but the truth is that we both got hurt."

He barked out a laugh. "Trust me, sugar. I'm not feeling too much sympathy for you at the moment."

"I get that, too. But have you thought about it

from my side? It's been almost five years, Winston. You thought I was dead, and that's horrible. And I'm so sorry I put you through that. But I was *dead*, at least as far as you knew."

She turned her head away, but not before he saw the tear snake down her cheek.

"Death happens all the time," she continued softly. "People go on with their lives. They heal. But me? I had to live my life knowing that you were right there, just a phone call or a drive or an airplane ride away, but I didn't even have the right to look at you. You think what I did is horrible? So do I. You think I hurt you? I know that I did. But I hurt me too. And believe me when I say it wasn't my choice."

His chest had tightened painfully, but when he spoke he worked to keep the emotion out of his voice. "Sweetheart, there's always a choice."

"Don't you get it? There was so much going on in Texas. Hades really was hell. You thought you saw the filth and corruption from your perspective as sheriff? You didn't even know the half of it."

She paused for a breath, and he had to remind himself to stay quiet. She didn't need to know that he'd been more than a small town sheriff. Not yet. Not until he'd heard the full story. The *real* story.

"They liked that I got close to you because you were the sheriff and I needed an in at the county. But our marriage was never an assignment, and I never expected to fall in love with you. Believe me, I wish I hadn't. It's turned out to be a painful inconvenience."

Her words lashed out at him like the flail of a whip.

She continued, her words tripping over each other. "But that wasn't the worst of it. I was undercover. Stuck in deep in the middle of the Consortium, one of the vilest groups we've ever taken down, and it was run all through that little town, like it was the center of a giant wheel. Hade's was the hub, and I was in the thick of it."

Her eyes flashed as she stared him down. "They killed hundreds of people. You only saw some of the bodies. Some of the dirt. Just a hint at how massive that operation was."

He stayed silent. He knew damn well the width and breadth of the Consortium.

"But we took them down, Winston." There was pride in her voice. Pride and power and regret, too. "The work I did undercover played a huge part in that. But there was a price."

He heard the pain in her voice, and his heart twisted. "You had to disappear."

She nodded. "Once the Consortium was under attack in Hades, they had to clear out. Deep cover, right? So I had to go with them. But they couldn't have some sheriff sniffing around like a dog with a bone. And you really were sniffing around. You caught that case, remember? It was a murder. And it led you into all sorts of places where you shouldn't have been looking."

He remembered. How could he forget?

"That case was what put you on the Consortium's map. Before that, you were more of an irritation. They needed you distracted and off the case."

"So they said you had to die."

"No. They said *you* did." She licked her lips. "They wanted you gone. They needed you to stop poking around. And I ... I begged them to save your life. They were going to kill you. They were going to take you out into the desert and put a bullet in the back of your head."

Tears trickled down her cheeks. "I pleaded with them to let you live. The Consortium was already wrapping up in Hades." Her words tumbled out on top of each other. "It was getting too hot. They were moving as much of their operation out as they possibly could."

She swallowed, then looked straight at him. "I had to do something fast. They wanted you gone or at least too distracted to pay attention. So I traded my life for yours."

"And it was easy for you." His voice was flat. "It was easy because you knew you'd be leaving me anyway. After all, I was only your cover while you were in town for your Hades operation."

"No!" Her voice was full of vehemence. "No,

you can't believe that. I would never have left you. I might never have told you the truth about the organization I worked for, but I would never have left you. The only reason I did is because they were going to kill you. And I couldn't bear the thought of you being dead, especially when I had a chance to save you."

He didn't know what to say. The words had the ring of truth about them. And it made sense that she thought she had to protect him from the big, bad Consortium.

After all, she'd truly believed he'd been just a small town sheriff. How could she have known that if she'd come to him they might have figured something out?

But she should have had faith. She should have believed that he had the skill or the resources to fight back. She'd owed him that, hadn't she? They'd been married, after all. Hell, they'd been happy.

And even if everything she said was true, how dare she make that big of a decision on her own? But even if it was wrong of her to decide, had her heart truly been in the right place? Or was she just yanking his chain right now, covering up the fact that she'd been nothing but a plant? A paper doll wife who'd been assigned to watch the local sheriff?

Frustrated, he turned away from her, his mind too full, and looking at her only made thinking harder, because he didn't want to believe their relationship had been a lie. God knows it hadn't been an act for him. And maybe, just maybe, it hadn't been an act for her, either. Her words—her tone— sure seemed to suggest that what they'd had in Hades was real.

Christ, he wanted to believe that. But they'd both lied to each other. Hell, their entire marriage had been built on lies, and she only knew the half of it.

But did that mean they both deserved the heartache? Maybe it did. If they hadn't deserved it, then life really was a damned unfair place because he'd been suffering for years, and even though he knew more about her than she was telling, something told him that she'd suffered, too.

Finally, he turned back around to face her. "All right. Keep going."

She gaped at him. "That's all you're going to say? No questions, no interrogation? No disbelief or arguing or asking me for details?"

"I told you to tell me your story. You're telling me your story. Or are you telling me *a* story?"

"I think you know what I'm telling you is the truth."

"So tell me the rest and let's see if you can keep up this streak of honesty."

She narrowed her eyes. "This really is incredibly uncomfortable. Would you please untie me? Cuff me to a chair. Make me wear the blanket and hide my clothes. Where would I go like that? But do I really have to stay here on the bed like this?"

"Yes."

"Fine," she snapped.

"Talk."

Her brow rose. "Oh, I'm happy to tell you the rest of it. Tomorrow." She yawned, so huge that it had him yawning in response. "I need to sleep now. Being in bed like this is making me so drowsy." She yawned again, then smiled. No, correction, she *smirked*.

"Linda..." He underscored her name with a warning tone.

"Don't worry, I'll tell you the rest after I've slept. And eaten. I never got my meal or my glass of wine." She smiled sweetly and batted her lashes. "Say what you will about him, but Bartlett was a much better date than you're turning out to be."

Despite himself, Winston laughed. On the bed, she grinned, too. "Come on, Winston. We both know you've got the upper hand here. I won't try to escape. Pinky swear."

He fought another smile, but lost. Well, fuck it.

He took a step toward her, pulling out his pocketknife as he did. He flipped it open, saw the quick flicker on her face as she watched the blade.

"Don't move." He stepped closer, then eased the knife in between her skin and the zip tie. It was the long, thick kind intended for industrial use, and he'd taken to carrying at least one on every mission after he'd lost a perp once.

The release tab was broken, and the plastic so thick that it took a bit of sawing with the knife for Winston to get her free. Once he did, though, she sat up, the blanket covering her breasts. She held her wrists in her lap and winced as she rubbed the tender flesh.

He grimaced. He hadn't intended to pull it that tight, and he regretted the red welts that now marred the soft skin of her wrists. He took one in his hand, rubbing his thumb lightly over the injury. "I'm sorry."

She yanked her hand away, and he felt like an ass, even though he truly wasn't the asshole here.

"I want food."

He nodded, wishing that the touch of her skin hadn't affected him so much—and that the way she'd yanked her arm away from him hadn't bothered him.

He cleared his throat. "Food, right." He lifted the handset and ordered burgers, fries, and wine from room service, his eyes never leaving her, and his free hand on the gun holstered at his hip.

"Less than fifteen minutes," he said after he hung up.

"Do I get to keep my hands and wrists free? Range of motion? Because I don't really want you shoving a burger in my mouth."

He considered the question. The truth was, he didn't doubt anything she'd said—at least not yet. But he hadn't heard the whole story. And he knew damn well that she was dangerous. He'd seen that clearly enough on a roof in Seattle.

She was Michelle Moon now, not Linda Starr. An assassin, not his wife. He'd do well to remember that.

"Hands free. Ankles tied to the chair. And you should know I have one in the chamber."

"You're the boss," she said curtly, then flashed a sweet smile. "At least for now."

He pointed toward the bathroom. "Robe," he said. "Let's go."

"Sure." She held his eyes as she pushed the blanket aside and stood up. She was naked, and though he didn't want it, he couldn't deny the way his body reacted to the sight of her.

She tilted her head and flashed him a flirtatious smile. "Too bad we're at odds," she said. "It's such a nice hotel room."

"In," he said, walking through the wide bathroom door with her, his hand on the butt of the gun, just in case.

A leather tote sat on the counter and her dress hung on one of two hooks behind the door, along with a hotel robe. She took a step toward the tote.

"No," he said. "Put on the robe." He pulled it down, checked the pockets, then handed it to her.

She lifted a shoulder as if to say *it was worth a try,* then slid her arms in. She turned to face him, the robe still open, revealing—well, revealing *everything.* And even though she'd been naked only moments before, somehow the subtle invitation of the open robe seemed more dangerous. On the bed, strapped down, he'd been in control.

Now, with her standing there in what seemed like a sultry invitation, it felt very much like the tables had just turned.

As if in acknowledgement, her eyes locked on his. For a moment she just stood like that, letting him see what used to be his. Letting him know what she'd be willing to trade for her freedom.

"Close the robe," he said, his voice cold. "And tie it. You don't have anything I'm interested in."

"We both know that's not true."

Lust curled through him, followed immediately by loathing. This was the woman who had walked away from him. Who'd had the opportunity to come tell him the truth later, but never did. The woman who now killed people for a living.

She wasn't the woman he'd known in Hades. He didn't know who she was. And he doubted he'd ever truly find out.

He shoved the emotions down, then used his free hand to grab her by the wrist. She gasped as he yanked her toward him, so that her body was pressed against his, her head tilted back and her eyes wide with surprise and, maybe, a bit of heat. But whether it was the heat of anger or desire, he didn't know.

For that matter, he didn't care. Because God knew this was never going to go anywhere. How could it? Whatever trust they'd had between them, real or fake, was completely gone now. And over the years, Winston had learned more and more that the most valuable thing in the world was trust.

He bent close to her ear and whispered, "I know what you do now, remember? I know you came here to kill. You aren't the woman I fell in love with. I don't know you at all. So don't think that you can flirt or play or tease your way out of this. It's not going to happen."

He pushed her back, studying her face. "Do you understand?"

Her eyes held a thousand questions as she studied him, but all she did was nod.

"Good. Table. Go."

She obeyed, turning and leaving the bathroom as he followed, the gun back in his shoulder holster. She passed the bed, then paused at the small cock-tail table by the balcony door. "Sit," he ordered, and she obeyed without hesitation or comment. He should be grateful. Instead, he wondered what mischief she was planning.

As soon as she was seated, he reached in his pocket for another zip tie, but there wasn't one. He frowned, trying to remember if the second one had fallen out when he'd attached her to the headboard. Dammit, he was off his game on this assignment. And the reason for that was standing in front of him wearing nothing but a bathrobe.

Hell. He unbuckled the belt and started to pull it off.

"Oh, sweetie, I don't think we have time before the food gets here," she said.

He shot her a scowl. "Hands stay on the table," he said as he bent and attached her leg to the chair with the belt, wrapping it multiple times before fastening it.

"Not on you?"

"Stop it." His voice came out like a lash. "It's not funny."

She recoiled, then dipped her eyes to the table-top. "No, you're right. Nervous habit."

Shit. He remembered that. She'd always made bad jokes when she was scared or nervous. "It's okay," he said. At least now he knew that he had her on edge. That gave him an advantage toward getting the truth.

He moved to his side of the table, then tapped the butt of the gun before sitting. "Don't get any ideas. I'm fast on the draw. And in case you've forgotten, I was a damn good shot when you knew me. Trust me when I say I've only gotten better."

"You always were an arrogant bastard."

He burst out laughing. "And that's one of the things I always enjoyed most about you. The way you always surprised me."

She looked at him then, completely deadpan. "Well, then, I suppose you must be loving today."

CHAPTER TEN

Room service was as good as its word, and they had food and wine within minutes. He kept her silverware and poured her wine, then sat back to enjoy his fries.

"What else do you want to know?" she asked, after taking a bite of the burger. "This is really good. Thank you."

He nodded, a bit surprised. "You're welcome. And, honestly, all I really want is the truth." He watched her face as he spoke. The dilation of her pupils. The way she didn't even blink.

"I've told you the truth," she said.

"Fine." He leaned back with a smile. "Convince me."

She shook her head, looking truly baffled. "How?"

"Details would be nice."

"I told you. I shouldn't have, but I did. I worked for the NSC and I was undercover with The Consortium."

"That's strike one, sugar. You want to be tied spread-eagled on that bed with no blanket and a lot of questions?"

Her brow rose and her voice was flirtatious as she asked, "Is that a promise or a threat?"

His entire body hardened from the image she'd just painted in his mind. Damn him, he didn't want that. Or her. Not anymore. Not knowing what he knew about who she really was.

Slowly, he let his gaze drift over her, ending at her eyes, certain that his own were hard and cold. "Do not play with me, Linda. I promise you this isn't a game."

When she swallowed, he knew he'd won that round. Her jaw tightened, and he imagined it was taking all her effort not to snap back a retort. He'd do it, and she had to know that. He'd never been a man for empty threats.

"I've already told you enough details to get me in deep shit. I worked for a division of the NSC. You don't believe me, call and ask. They'll tell you I went on leave after my husband died." She practically snarled the words.

"So you worked for the Consortium, and your cover was that you were a clerk in the mayor's offices. But really, you were a deep cover NSC operative the whole time."

"Finally. I was starting to think I'd have to paint you a picture."

"Go on. Explain to me why I didn't know any of this back then."

"There are rules, Winston. You worked in law enforcement. Sometimes there are secrets, and they're sacrosanct for a reason. Because if you spill a secret, someone can get killed." She met his gaze, held it. "Someone you love."

"Don't talk to me about love," he snapped, but he didn't look away. Damn it all, even now he wanted to get lost in her eyes. Wanted to brush his thumb over her bottom lip and remember its softness one last time.

He wanted to touch her—and he hated himself for craving what he couldn't have. More important, what he shouldn't want. She was a liar, an assassin, and a traitor. To the country and to every sense of decency he'd once thought they'd shared.

"There are people out there," she continued. "People who trade on power, who trade on pain. People who work in the underbelly. People who do things like torch a car and kill an innocent woman without a second thought. Back then, you didn't even question that it happened to me because you knew that it could. And so much worse."

His gut twisted, not because she spoke the

truth, but because of the memory that her words invoked. The pain of that day. The horror of seeing what he had believed they'd done to his wife.

Yes, she was right. He'd never doubted that she'd died in that car. Never rebelled and yelled that people couldn't do that to one another. Of course they could. He'd seen it dozens of times, so often he'd become numb to it.

But he hadn't been numb that day. He'd hurt right down to the bone. Honestly, he still did.

"Some people don't have a soul," she continued, almost as if she were reading his thoughts. "And every time I went against them, every time I took one out, it chipped away at my own soul too. But it was worth it, because it was important."

She lifted her chin. "So there you go. And it doesn't matter if you believe that or not. It's still the truth." She held his gaze, her eyes dark and firm. He nodded. It was a concession he hadn't intended to give her, but she deserved to know that, at least in this regard, they were on the same page.

"Is that still what you believe?"

"Of course," she said.

"Are you still working for the NSC?"

"No. I told you. I do clerical work now. It's dull, but I had my fill of excitement years ago."

"Right."

He watched the confusion wash over her face.

He let her wonder for a while then said, "Convenient, don't you think?"

She frowned. "What do you mean?"

"Well, you said I could call the NSC, but that's not really possible. Organizations like the NSC or the Consortium tend to keep their former and current employee list secret, even from former sheriffs."

She exhaled. "For fuck's sake, Winston. What is it you think you know? What are you digging for?"

"Just the truth, darlin'. Just the truth."

She lifted her hands and let them drop, then turned her attention to her dinner.

He let the silence linger, but she didn't take the bait. Just dragged a french fry through ketchup, then ate it. Then another, and another.

And she didn't say a thing.

He had to give her credit. There were very few people who could withstand the power of silence.

He waited another three minutes, then broke the silence himself. "Been to Seattle lately?"

He kept his eyes on her as he spoke, and he had to admit that she was good. Very good. She didn't react at all. At least not so that a casual observer would see. But he knew her well, and he thought that maybe—just maybe—the corner of her eyes had crinkled in surprise.

He hoped so. He wanted her to know he was

dangerous. And that she didn't know him as well as she thought she had.

"Well?" he pressed.

"I was in Seattle not long ago. Why do you ask?"

"I think you know."

She rolled her eyes. "No. I don't. I had a meeting." She shrugged, casual and easy. "Beyond that, I don't know what you're talking about."

"Then let me be more specific. You killed a man in cold blood. And now you've come here, to Austin, to kill Tommy Bartlett."

_____

CHAPTER ELEVEN

F*uck. Fuck, fuck, fuck.*

The curse slams through my head even as I frown, furrow my brow as if confused, and say, "I don't know what you're talking about. You called me a killer for hire earlier, and now you're saying I came here to kill the guy I picked up on a dating app? I told you the truth—I used to be in intelligence. And, yeah, I've had to kill people in the line of duty. But that is *not* who I am."

To my ears, I sound convincing. But I know perfectly well I haven't convinced Winston of anything. The man knows too much.

"Do not play games with me," he says. "I really don't have the patience."

"Look, I get that you're angry and that you don't trust me. Honestly, I don't blame you. But I am not in the spy business anymore. I met Bartlett on a dating app. If you think it was some sort of pre-arranged meet, then somebody else is pulling my strings."

He exhales, sounding so exhausted and frustrated that I almost want to reach across the table and pat him on the shoulder.

"I'm not going to play games," he says. "It's time to lay all my cards on the table."

"Great," I say. "Clarity would be nice, because right now, I don't know what the hell is going on." Another easy lie. After so many years, I barely have to think about it anymore. And with every day that goes by, I become less and less sure that's a good thing.

"Tommy Bartlett's an accountant. And he has some information on that laptop over there that could put Billy Hawthorne and his people behind bars for a very long time. Bartlett's the only person who can access that incredibly encrypted machine. But he's agreed to do that and testify in exchange for immunity."

"Really?" I feign surprise. "Sounds like a good deal for him. I imagine Billy Hawthorne's pretty pissed off." In truth, I don't have to imagine it at all. I was standing not three feet away when Billy hurled one of his chrome and leather chairs through a plate glass window with a stunning view of Lake Erie.

"Oh, he's pissed off, all right," Winston says.

"Mad enough to hire someone to kill Bartlett and recover the laptop. No evidence, no testimony. And Hawthorne's organization continues to limp along until another opportunity comes along for an agent to get a foot in the door."

He studies my face again, frowning.

I know he's playing me, and I should ignore it. But I say, "What?"

"Just wondering if this sounds familiar."

"Not really."

"No? Because the word on the street is that you're the assassin Hawthorne hired."

"Really? And exactly what street is that? Because I'm thinking you need a new map."

To his credit, Winston chuckles. But when he turns serious, it's deadly. I can see it in his eyes. "We're done with play time," he says. "Right now, you can keep denying and pretending ignorance or you can tell me the truth. Those are your only options. In fact, it's even simpler than that. The bottom line is this—you're going to tell me the truth or you're not leaving this room alive."

My pulse starts to race, and I force myself to breathe before answering. To take control. To reclaim this conversation. "You won't kill me," I tell him. "I know you too well. I know the kind of man you are. There's no way you would do that."

His smile is slow and confident and deeply scary. "Trust me, Linda, the man you used to know is long gone. The Winston sitting here with you? You don't know him at all. Honestly, he's pretty damn pissed."

I force myself not to react. He could be bluffing. Years ago, I would have known for sure. Now, I don't know shit.

So I do the only thing I can do—I shift the conversation. "I know a little bit, too," I tell him. "For one thing, you've got a lot of information for a man supposedly out of the business. So what exactly are you doing these days, Winston, hmm? Because I have a feeling you've never been on a movie set in your life."

"A couple of times, actually," he says.

"Really?" My interest is genuine, and I don't bother to modulate my tone.

He shrugs. "I live in LA now. And I have some friends who are connected."

"How fun."

We share a smile. Winston's parents are classic movie fiends, and I love anything Hollywood. Hades had a four-plex cinema at the edge of town. Two new releases and two-dollar shows, and hitting the theater on Wednesdays and Fridays was the anchor of our routine. That, and what came after once we got home.

My body responds with the memory, and I glance down at our half-eaten meal so he won't see my face. But to my surprise, his voice is tender when he says, "Yeah. I know. Me, too."

I look up, and for a moment, we've traveled back in time. "I'm sorry," I say, as if we'd just had a stupid fight about loading the dishwasher. "I'm so, so sorry."

He nods, then swallows. Even in the dim light, I can see that his eyes are damp. "What did you do after?" he asks, and even though there's no context whatsoever, I know what he's asking.

"I left town. I couldn't stay. If I—If I'd seen you, I wouldn't have been able to leave."

He nods slowly. "So you didn't come to your funeral. Would've been interesting."

"No. I wouldn't have been able to bear it. Seeing you, but not talking to you." I close my eyes and shake my head. "No."

"The Consortium fell apart soon after. I know, because I took out most of the players personally."

"I know. They told me."

"Of course they did." He holds on tight to the edge of the table, and I'm pretty sure he's fighting the urge to throw his plate against the wall just for the cathartic pleasure of watching it shatter. "I was in a rage," he says, his voice hardening under the emotion. "I used it as a lever for finishing them off."

"Nothing like that is ever truly dead. Billy Hawthorne's the one who moved in to pick up the pieces."

"And now you work for him. What am I supposed to think about that?"

"I keep telling you that your information is wrong. I'm not Billy Hawthorne's hired gun."

He scoffs.

"I know you don't believe me, but it's true. Based on what you know—or what you *knew*—do you really think I'd work for the likes of him?" I'm coming dangerously close to breaking rules that I believe in. Shattering confidences and breaking vows.

Hell, I'm coming dangerously close to treason.

But I gave up everything so that this man could live. Maybe it's selfish, but I think the universe owes me a pass.

"We both know people change," he says. "It's not always for the better."

"I haven't," I promise him. "Not like that."

His body sags, almost as if he's exhausted. "I know what I've seen."

"And what's that?"

"Drone footage. A roof in Seattle. You. A man. And a single shot to the head."

I can't help it; I wince.

"And I know that the hit was authorized by Hawthorne. The same way he authorized the hit on Bartlett. Your boss is going to be pissed when he finds out you let his prey run free."

"You really believe that?"

"I saw it. And we both know why Hawthorne wants Bartlett dead, and here you are, ready to carry out the orders."

"No."

"No, what?"

Shit. I draw a breath, because if I tell him the rest of it, I really will be falling down the rabbit hole. But I loved Winston Starr once, and I need him to know the truth. Vows, promises, and oaths be damned.

I'm dead, after all. And I'm pretty sure that the dead aren't expected to keep their promises.

"So I guess I was right about you," I say.

"About me?"

"You are in the game."

A muscle in his cheek twitches. "Is that what we're playing? I show you mine, you show me yours?"

I bat my eyes and flash a flirtatious smile. "Could be fun," I say, and to my relief, he smiles. "They recruited you," I say. "After you went renegade and did the heavy lifting for them, they recruited you into the NSC or something."

He shakes his head. "No." He draws a breath. "Full disclosure—I was always in."

I lean back, processing those words. "And by *in*, you mean what?"

"The sheriff job was a cover. I was with the SOC. Sensitive—"

"—Operations Command," I say, feeling queasy. "I know what it is, you goddamn hypocrite."

His eyes go wide. "I never faked my death. If we're keeping score, I still win."

"Shit." I push myself up because I want to pace, then remember that I'm strapped to the damn chair. I start to bend over so that I can undo the buckle, but his voice stops me cold.

"Sit back down."

I glance back to find him aiming that damn Glock at me. "Seriously?"

"We are not five by five yet. Not by a long shot. I work for the SOC. My work is sanctioned. You're taking assassination orders from Billy Hawthorne. Guess which one of us is walking the moral high ground."

"You are in way over your head," I tell him.

He sits up straight, his shoulders rolling back. "You're the one who said I was in the game. And I agreed with you. Even told you what agency I'm associated with. Showing our cards, remember?"

"And now that I've seen your cards, I have to tell you that this isn't Amateur Hour." I lick my lips. "I don't want to see you get hurt. Or worse."

"I'm no amateur, sugar, and meeting you here was no coincidence. My assignment is to recover Bartlett's laptop and stop his assassination. Looks like I managed that. And I'll reacquire the accountant soon enough."

"Assignment," I repeat, so softly I'm not even sure he hears me. "Oh, fuck me. Of course. Winston, you have to listen to me. I know you think I'm bluffing, but if you ever loved me at all, you need to believe me, or you will end up well and truly fucked."

His eyes narrow, and though I'm sure he thinks I'm only playing games, he says, "What the hell are you talking about?"

"Seagrave's dirty," I tell him, my pulse pounding hard. "And the information on that laptop proves it."

CHAPTER TWELVE

W inston rocked back as if her words had been a slap. "Are you insane?"

"He's the reason I'm here. In this hotel. Tracking down Bartlett."

His head was spinning, and he wanted to kick himself. She'd drawn him in. Spun a nice tale of a girl trapped in a bad circumstance. A woman who'd fallen in love while working a deep cover op. And, dammit, he'd believed her.

But now this?

She was yanking his chain, and it was bullshit.

"Where's your proof?"

"Proof? I just laid it at your feet. Actually, you laid it at mine."

"What are you talking about?"

She tried to get up, remembered the belt around her leg, and sat back down in a huff. "You're here to take me out. To get the laptop. To bring Bartlett safely in."

"Yes."

"To Seagrave. Your boss."

"Well, he's not actually my boss, but yes," he said again, twirling his hand so that she'd get to the point.

Instead, she asked, "What do you mean he's not your boss?"

He almost didn't answer, but he was the one who said they were putting their cards on the table. "I'm not actually with the SOC anymore. I quit after you—well, after I thought you died. These days I work out of a private security agency based in Los Angeles."

"What agency?"

"Stark Security."

She nodded, looking genuinely impressed. "They've got a good rep."

"Deservedly so. And I don't think Anderson Seagrave is duping Damien Stark or Ryan Hunter any more than he's duping me."

"Don't be naive," she said, her tone suggesting that she was rolling her eyes even though her face remained entirely passive. "You can't assess someone that way. You like the guy? So what? Traitors, serial killers, psychopaths. Some of the most notorious ones in history were very, very likable."

He didn't argue, because he couldn't. She was

right.

But he still couldn't believe it was true.

"Come on, Winston," she said gently. "Think about it. There are at least a dozen operational commanders at the SOC. You never told me which one you work with. And yet I knew. How? Because he's the crux of *my* mission."

The words slammed against him with the force of an elephant's kick, knocking him back. "No," he said, even as he remembered the terror in Bartlett's eyes as Winston had said Seagrave's name. As if he was looking at the Angel of Death.

He shook his head, pushing the thoughts aside. "No way. That laptop shows the flow of money through Hawthorne to a government agent, you're right about that being true. But not the SOC. Seagrave needs the laptop and Bartlett to prove who really is dirty."

"I don't know anything about payoffs," she said. "But it sounds to me like he's telling you the truth you need to hear. He's just not telling you that *he's* the dirty agent."

"No. I know this man. I've worked with him for years. Hell, I worked with him when I was on the Hades mission. He came to our wedding."

Her eyes went wide. "Our wedding? What are you talking about?"

"Uncle Andy."

Her hand fluttered to her mouth. "In the

wheelchair?"

He nodded. It had been risky having Seagrave there, but he'd wanted real friends. Emma and Seagrave had come, and so had his parents and brother, who'd believed he was the sheriff marrying a nice local girl.

And since Linda had no family, Uncle Andy had even given her away.

She reached across the table and took his hand, and for the first time since he'd seen her, he wanted to simply hold on, sharing his strength. He didn't trust her, not yet. Not really.

But he couldn't deny that he wanted to.

And that, he knew, made her all the more dangerous.

Slowly, he tugged his hand back, breaking their contact. He took a moment to gather himself, then lifted his face to hers. "Seagrave isn't dirty. I know it."

"No," she said simply. "You don't. You can't." She cocked her head. "Unless it's you who's dirty. Then I guess you'd actually know the truth."

"Dammit, Linda—"

"Look, this is the entire basis of my mission. Bartlett hired me for the hit, sure. But I'm not going to go around assassinating his enemies."

Winston crossed his arms over his chest. "Seattle."

"That bastard was responsible for the bombing

of two elementary schools in Europe that he staged to look like US military actions. It was a hit sanctioned at the highest level."

"Which, of course, I have no way to confirm."

She shrugged. "Sorry about that."

"Fine. Go on. Tell me something else I can't confirm."

She shot him a scowl so familiar it made his heart twist with the memory.

"What's wrong?"

"Nothing. Go ahead."

"Fine. As I was saying, I never carry out Hawthorne's orders directly. I run them through my handler and work the counter mission. With the bomb guy, it was a termination, but that's rare. Usually we'll fake a death then put the target in witness protection."

"You're telling me Bartlett was going under at the government's expense?"

"No, no. That's what I anticipated. But my handler told me to take him out. He said the information in Bartlett's head and on that computer was too sensitive."

"Accounting info."

"No," she said. "That's the point. The laptop doesn't really have accounting information. What's in those files is the identity of deep cover agents all over the globe. Can you imagine how much that would be worth on the black market?"

"And you know this because...?"

"Obviously it's been a long-term mission at my division. And Collins has been overseeing it since—"

"Collins?" he said. "Dustin Collins?"

Her brow furrowed as she studied him. "Yes. Why?"

"You're with ID-9."

Her eyes went wide. "How the hell do you know about ID-9?"

He exhaled, then dragged his fingers through his hair. "Because, darlin', your Mr. Collins is the son of a bitch that Bartlett's going to testify against."

"What?" She shook her head. "No, that can't be."

"It is."

"And you know this because Seagrave told you."

He tilted his head. "And Collins told you."

She closed her eyes. "Fuck."

"That about sums it up."

She started to rise, then cursed when her leg caught. She sat down hard, then held up a hand. "Give me a sec to think."

"Hell, I need a second, too."

After a moment, she took a long swallow of wine, then said, "We need to find Bartlett. Find him, then we see what's on his laptop ourselves."

It wasn't a bad idea, Winston thought. Except for one little problem. "No," he said.

She gaped at him. "No?"

"How can I ensure that this isn't a full-blown secondary protocol for you to reacquire Bartlett and take him out?"

"You aren't serious."

"It would be exactly the kind of next-level planning a division like ID-9 would put in place."

"Winston, this is absurd. I can't prove a negative. You're locking us into doing nothing. Are we supposed to just sit here until Bartlett decides to come back? Because that's not happening."

"We have the laptop."

"It's not hackable."

"I have some very smart friends."

She dragged her fingers through her hair. "Weren't you briefed? That laptop has every sort of countermeasure imaginable. One wrong move and the information is erased."

"That's good if it's full of the names of deep cover agents."

"And bad if it also erases evidence of who collected those names in the first place," she shot back. "Or if it's not agents at all, but accounting information, just like you said. Payouts for information leaks. Do we really want to risk losing that kind of evidence?"

"We don't," Winston admitted. "But I think we're at an impasse."

"Shit."

He chuckled.

"What?" she snapped.

"The last time we fought like this it was about whether or not to screen in the back porch. I won."

"Yeah, well I'm winning tonight."

"I don't think so. In fact I—*what the hell?*"

He didn't even have time to think as she shoved the table over on its side and leaped forward, her leg still tied to the chair. Then he was on his back and she was on top of him. Linda *and* the chair.

But the thing that really concerned him was the broken wine glass she held at his throat.

"Will you agree with me that I have more experience in the field with terminations?"

He grunted his agreement.

"And will you agree that right now, I could cut your jugular and there's not a damn thing you could do except bleed out?"

"Linda—"

"Do you agree?"

He closed his eyes and made a concerted effort not to swallow. "Yes," he said, opening his eyes again and meeting her hard gaze. "At the moment, you have the upper hand."

"Good. Thank you." She tossed the glass aside, then bent sideways and unbuckled his belt, releasing her leg from the chair. "Object lesson over. Just trust me already, okay?"

He sat up, groaning from the ache in his back. "Trust you, huh? About what, exactly?"

"Something's not right."

He shot her a narrow look, and she grinned.

"Yeah, yeah," she said as she climbed to her feet. "But if we're both telling the truth—what we think is the truth, anyway—then one of us was duped."

"So we work together," he finished. "We find Bartlett. We figure out which one of our bosses is bad."

She nodded. "Or if you want an alternative plan, we can pretend I gave you the slip." She moved around the rubble of the table to the balcony. She slid open the door, then stood there silhouetted against the downtown Austin skyline, the twinkle of lights making the white of the bathrobe glow.

She looked back over her shoulder. "You can walk out of here if you want. I'll figure this out, and you can go back to the SOC and report in to Seagrave that Bartlett never showed up. After all, it's not really your problem. Not officially."

"It's my problem," he said, joining her in the doorway. "Someone in intelligence is selling information. Maybe about deep cover agents, maybe about something else. But whatever it is, it's a breach of trust, and it matters. I'm not going to stand for that."

Her smile warmed his soul. "I'm glad to see that despite everything, you're still the man I remember."

"So we're working together?" he asked.

She nodded. "We are."

He knew he shouldn't, but he couldn't help himself. His hand seemed to rise of its own accord as he brushed her cheek, then cupped the back of her head.

"Winston," she whispered as he pulled her close.

He waited. Just a heartbeat, but it was enough time for her to pull back. Except she didn't. She stayed there, her eyes looking deep into his. Her lips parted in invitation.

And so he kissed her, this woman he'd kissed so many times in his dreams and memories. The woman he'd never expected to feel again in his arms. The woman he'd once loved with all his soul, who'd fired his senses, who'd made him laugh.

She was back in his arms, and the world seemed filled with light.

At least until she stepped back and he saw the errant tears on her cheeks.

"Oh, sugar, what is it?"

"I'm sorry," she whispered, the words cracking his soul. "But we can't."

CHAPTER THIRTEEN

"Can't," he repeats, taking a step back from me. "Of course not. I shouldn't have—"

"I want to," I admit. "But—but I don't want to confuse things."

"Confuse things," he repeats. "Are you with someone? God, are you married?"

"No. God no." I reply with more vehemence than the question calls for, and I try to dial it back in. "It's just that this—finding each other again like this—I, I didn't expect it. And right now, I don't have the bandwidth to process it. We need to find Bartlett. And on top of that, we need to check in with our respective handlers."

For a moment, he simply stands there as if he has no idea what I'm talking about. Then he squeezes the bridge of his nose and looks at me hard.

"What?"

"You mess with my head," he says. "Seeing you again. Touching you. I think you've re-wired my brain. You're right, of course. Somehow being around you again has completely erased my ability to think clearly."

I flash a watery smile. "I know the feeling."

"Truce?" He holds out his hand, and I take it, and the shock of that simple connection ricochets through me, making me crave things I shouldn't want. Things I can't have. The touch of his hand, the brush of his lips. I want to talk with him the way we used to. I want a past that is gone, a man that I can't have, and a love I don't deserve.

Except we never really had those things. We were actors playing house. It was warm and comfortable and wonderful, but it was never truly real.

I let go, feigning nonchalance, then slip my hands in the pockets of the robe as I glance at the clock on the bedside table. "We both should have checked in already," I say again.

"Will Collins wonder why you're late?"

I shake my head. "I've worked with Collins since before Hades. He trusts me. For that matter, I trust him."

"That doesn't mean he's not dirty."

"I know. I'm the one who said that to you. But I still hate this whole situation."

His eyes meet mine. "I don't. Most of it, yes. But part of this situation is a gift."

His words slide over me, his voice like the most intimate caress. "Winston, please. We need—"

"What?"

"We need to figure this out. *This*," I stress. "Not us. Not right now," I add, to soften the blow.

His face tightens, but he nods in acknowledgment. "What about Hawthorne?"

"We're clean there, too. He'll be in a fury when I tell him, but I'm positive he doesn't already know. That's not how he works. What about on your side of things?"

"I trust Seagrave," he says, mimicking my response about Collins. I take the cue and roll my eyes.

"I've worked with him since before Hades, too," he continues. He exhales loudly. "Hell, maybe they're both clean as a whistle. But we won't know until we know."

"I'm not arguing. And, again, I'm going to say that this situation sucks."

"Amen to that." He bends to pick up the table that I knocked over when attacking him. "Nice maneuver, by the way."

"You should have seen it coming. That was sloppy of you."

He looks at me over the newly-righted table. "Maybe I wanted to test my wife. See how far she'd go to get free, and whether she would have actually hurt me."

I meet his eyes and allow myself the tiniest of smiles. "I don't like being trapped."

He studies my face, then nods. "Fair enough. I don't blame you."

I look away, uncomfortable with the intense way he's looking at me, as if he's trying to read almost five years of lost emotions in my eyes.

"There's a tracker," I say. "On Bartlett."

"You're serious?"

I nod. "I slipped it into his jacket pocket when I got to the bar. I expected he'd invite me to his room, but just in case, I wanted a backup plan."

"Let's go get the son of a bitch."

"I can track him on my phone," I say, turning toward the bathroom, where I'd left the leather tote I use as both a purse and an operational kit.

He follows me, and I sit in front of the dressing table and pull the tote onto my lap. My hands brush my gun.

"I'm carrying," I say. "Glock 9mm." I'm not sure why it seems important to tell him, but if we're going in together, I want to show all my cards.

"Good for you," he says nonchalantly. "Better than the rough end of a wine glass. Although you might want to holster it."

I nod. "I've got a change of clothes in the back of my rental car. And we should get a new vehicle once we know where we're heading. Odds are good ID-9 will keep tabs on mine."

I've been rummaging for my phone, and I pull it out now, then open the tracking app. "Airport," I say.

"Shit."

"Airport *hotel*," I clarify. "Probably booked on something tomorrow."

"Come on." He stands, and I glance down at the bathrobe I'm wearing. "Right," he says with a chuckle. "Although I do like the way that looks on you."

I point toward the dress I wore to the bar, now hanging on the back of the door. "Gimme," I say, and he tosses it to me as I stand. "I'll wear this now and change when we switch cars."

I'm about to let the robe drop to the floor when I realize what I'm doing. "Can you—I mean, give me a moment, okay?"

"Right. Sorry. I wasn't thinking. Old habits."

I smile weakly; I know what he means. It's like muscle memory around Winston, and part of me wants nothing more than to give in to it. But I can't. Because the past is gone. And there's no way to go back to it. No way to move forward from that once upon a time when we were together and happy.

Those days are behind us, and the love we shared never really existed at all. The happiness we've both mourned so deeply is tainted with the stain of lies, both his and mine.

And I'm not sure there's any power in the universe that can clean up a stain that dark.

"The bastard didn't show," I tell Collins.

"Am I on speaker? What the hell, Moon?"

"Cut me some slack. I'm in a bitch of a mood." Not true, but I want Winston to hear Collins' voice, too. If he's lying or suspicious, I don't want to miss those telltale tones.

"Don't worry," I add. "The phone's a secure line, and I swept the room. No listening devices. I'm checking his suitcase now. I need both hands if I don't want him to know I was here. I haven't found the laptop. He must have it on him."

Collins makes a grunting noise. "I want that computer."

"But you want Bartlett out of the picture more."

"No. Both. This is a two-prong assignment. You're clear on that?"

"Crystal."

"You think he got wind of who you are? Is that why he bailed?"

I glance at Winston. His head is tilted to one side, his eyes closed as he listens intently. "Highly unlikely," I tell Collins. "He called the bar and left me a message. He's running late and hoping I can join him for an after-dinner drink."

"Which you will, of course."

"With bells on."

"And Hawthorne? This is his assignment. Have you checked in with him?"

"No, sir. You know his protocol."

"You know you're more to him than a hired gun. You need to build that relationship."

"I'm aware of that, sir."

Collins sighs. "I'm not trying to whore you out," he says, and I watch as Winston's brow rises. "But I want Hawthorne in a box. He's putting the lives of our agents and our national security at risk."

"I know, sir. This is just a change in timing, not an abort of the mission. I'll report in as soon as the target is eliminated and the laptop secure."

"All right then. And good luck, Moon. The men and women working undercover around the globe are relying on you."

"Thank you, sir," I say, then end the call. I wait a moment, then turn my phone off entirely, mostly because it's in my job description to be paranoid. I look at Winston. "Your take?"

"If he's a traitor, he's a damn good actor."

I nod. I appreciate the honesty, but he doesn't look happy about it. "Your turn."

"Right," he says, then dials Anderson Seagrave's secure line.

"Starr," Seagrave says after the preliminaries. "I hope you're telling me that you have Bartlett and Moon in custody and a laptop in evidence."

"Not yet, sir. Just wanted to update you. The target's meet was changed, but I've got eyes on Moon," he adds as I curtsy, holding out the skirt of the dress and dipping like a debutante. I immediately regret it, as he almost laughs. "I'll update you soon," he says, his voice sounding only a little choked.

"I do have one question, though," Winston continues. "If the SOC is that close to convincing him to testify, wouldn't it be better to bring in an agent to negotiate those terms, get him secured, and transport him back to LA?"

"If he wasn't a walking target, I'd agree with you. But Moon's presence has made the situation more difficult. He'll understand that he was brought in as a protective measure. And once he realizes he was only inches away from assassination —and we saved him—he'll be even more likely to finalize his deal and testify."

He glances at me, and I nod. It was a good question, but Seagrave's response makes sense.

"A curtsy?" he says to me once he's ended the call. "You're going to get us in trouble."

I try to look somber, but I can't help it. The

day's been too damn stressful. I burst into laughter, and he joins me, taking my hand and pulling me close. For a moment, we stay like that, even though I know I should pull away. I was the one who said this was too confusing, after all.

Except I can't seem to move. The moment is sweet, almost gentle, and I want to soak it up. I want to wrap myself in our shared memories. But then the tension shifts between us to something more intense. A crackling heat. A bold intensity. A sensual temptation that looms in front of me like a dark pool of warm water, beckoning me to dive in. And I want to. Oh, God, I really want to.

I don't.

Instead, I clear my throat and step back, glancing at his face only long enough to see the flicker of disappointment quickly wiped away by a professional facade.

I know he doesn't understand. I'm not sure I do. All I know is that despite the fact that the attraction still burns between us as bright as a supernova, giving in to it would be a mistake.

"I didn't hear anything odd in Seagrave's voice," I say, as if the air wasn't still thick with tension. "Did you?"

"No." His voice is vague, but his gaze is intense, like he's searching me for secrets. He clears his throat. "No. Nothing off at all."

"Well, it was a long shot to think we'd be able to

judge by their tone. And the odds of one of them telling us the mission needs to succeed so that they can continue to hide their dirty little secret were pretty damn low."

"Especially when the house always wins."

I shake my head. "No. We're the house, because we're the good guys. We're going to figure this out." I start to bend over for my tote, but he takes my elbow, tugging me back up.

"And then what?"

"Then we talk to the US Attorney and see about prosecuting."

"No. That's not what I mean."

My shoulders sag. "I know," I admit. "But Winston," I say, "I just don't know."

CHAPTER FOURTEEN

"Tell me you are *not* calling Stark Security," Linda said, frowning as he pulled out his phone.

They were in her rented Toyota, heading through East Austin toward the highway that led to the local airport. She'd changed into jeans, a V-neck tee, and a blazer to cover the shoulder holster. Her hair was pulled back into a ponytail with only wisps left to dance around her face. She looked as young and beautiful as she had when he'd first seen her in Hades, and if it weren't for the fact that they had an asshole to track, Winston would have happily passed the day staring at her.

Instead, apparently he was going to argue with her.

"Do you trust me?"

If brows could rise sarcastically, hers did. "Isn't

that the point of our truce?" she asked, as she pulled to a stop for a red light. "Trust each other, find the bad guys? But that doesn't include pulling someone into this clusterfuck who might be in bed with Seagrave."

"I'm calling Emma. Well, you knew her as Emily."

He watched her brow furrow. "Emily from Hades? The mayor's assistant after that scrawny guy quit?"

"That's her." Although he'd used his real first name, Emma had opted to switch it up.

She shook her head, frowning. "Another under-cover operative."

"She was with the SOC during the Hades operation, too. We've worked quite a few jobs together. Now she's at Stark Security. She's a friend and I trust her. She's not in this," he said firmly. "If Seagrave is dirty, she's not a part of it."

"And you know this because...?"

"Because I know her."

She licked her lips, then swallowed. "You knew me, too."

The words were like a knife to his heart.

"Yes." He heard the crack in his voice and hated himself for it. "And unless I made a very foolish deal, I can trust you now. Or am I wrong?"

"No," she said softly. "You're not wrong." She reached for his hand, only to draw it back at the last minute and return it firmly to the steering wheel. "I'm sorry. I shouldn't have said that. I don't want you second-guessing people because of me. But I also don't want to trust the wrong person and then find out we've walked into a trap."

"That makes two of us."

He watched her shoulders rise and fall as she drew a deep breath. For a moment she said nothing. Then she offered him a quick, curt nod. "All right, then. If you're sure about her, call. God knows we can use all the help we can get."

"I'm as sure about her as I am about you," he said.

She turned and caught his eye. "I hope that means you're going to call."

"It does," he said. "And I damn sure hope I'm not fooling myself about either of you."

Her smile didn't quite reach her eyes, and as he dialed Emma's number, he hoped she realized that his promise of trust wasn't a ruse. He couldn't go halfway on this mission. Couldn't be looking over his shoulder waiting for the other shoe to drop. They'd made a pact, and he was going to honor it.

If he'd been a fool, he supposed he'd find that out in the long run. Right now, he could only do what he could do.

Emma answered on the first ring, her laughter filling the car as she said, "No, no, stop, you fiend!

Winston doesn't want to hear—oh, shit. Hey, guy. I
didn't realize the call had connected."

"Sorry to interrupt."

"No interruption. We're just watching a
movie."

"Uh-huh."

"Pinkie swear," she said, and he had to laugh.

"I'm with Linda," he said. "You're on speaker."

For a moment, silence lingered. Then Emma
cleared her throat. "So I guess we were right. Your
mission did have to do with her."

"Yeah," Winston said. "You could say that."

"Okay. Right. Well, I'm sure there's some
etiquettely correct way of saying hello to a dead
woman, but I've never been big with the manners.
So, you know, hey there, Linda."

"Good to hear your voice, too, Em," Linda said
dryly.

To her credit, Emma laughed, though it
sounded a bit strained. "And everything is
copacetic?"

"I don't have a gun pressed to his temple if
that's what you mean," Linda said.

"Wasn't aware that was a concern," Emma
countered. "But good information to have.
Winston," she continued, her voice tight, "you want
to tell me what's going on?"

"I can't give you the details," Winston said,
"but Linda and I have a truce. We considered cele-

brating by swinging by some divey restaurant for a few hotdogs, but decided to chase a bad guy instead."

"Gotcha." Emma's voice softened, losing the knife-edge and gaining a note of humor. "In that case, tell me how I can help."

The corner of Linda's mouth twitched. "Divey or hotdog?" she asked, and both Emma and Winston laughed. Of course she'd recognized the use of a code word to reassure Emma that Winston wasn't speaking under duress.

"I could tell you," Winston said in a deadpan voice. "But then I'd have to kill you."

"Funny man." Linda shot him a smile so genuine that it made his heart flip. Then she shifted her head, talking toward the phone the way people do. "We need you to check airline records. We're looking for a specific passenger. Either on a flight in the last few hours or booked to take off soon. Possibly registered at the airport hotel."

"I'll need a name."

"Tommy Bartlett," Linda said.

"Hang on, let me get to my computer."

A moment passed, and when her voice came back, Winston added, "Emma, we need you to keep this to yourself. No word of it to Seagrave or the SOC. No word to anyone at Stark Security."

"I'm alone now, but Tony's in bed and naked. I

mean, I can probably distract him if he asks questions, but..."

"I can't even tell you how much I did not need to know that. Just don't volunteer information. I called to update you on my mission. Just me. Not me and Linda."

"No problem."

"I hate to ask you to keep something from him," he added. "I wouldn't normally, but it's—"

"Oh, please. Give me some credit."

"Pardon?" Winston said. Behind the wheel, Linda sat up straighter, looking a little smug.

"It goes with the job," Emma said. "Secrets, I mean. It's nothing personal. I know that. You know it. Tony knows it. Just give me a sec."

Winston nodded slowly, soaking up her words. He knew it all right. He just wasn't sure he'd actually been living it.

"Okay, I'm back," Emma said, her words underscored by the clicking of keys. "Not finding him on any airline manifests ... hang on, hang on ... oh, fuck you, God, I hate technology."

Beside him, Linda bit back a laugh, then reached for his hand. Their fingers brushed, and then she looked down. Her lips parted, and she mouthed, "Sorry," before tugging her fingers back.

He nodded like it was no big deal, but it was. One simple, unthinking touch, and it brought back a flood of longing so intense it felt like a physical weight bearing down on him.

To cover, he reached for the water bottle in the console, then took a long sip as he scoped out the area. They were on Highway 71 now, almost to the exit for the airport. As far as he was concerned, they couldn't get there fast enough. He wanted out of this car. Needed to be moving and working. At the very least, he needed just a hint of space between them. Because while his head might be fully with the we're-just-working-together pact, his body craved a full reconciliation. Or maybe just closure.

Hell, he didn't know. All he knew was that he still wanted her. And damned if that wasn't distracting as hell.

"No luck," Emma said, the words a welcome interruption to his jumbled thoughts. "Not on any flight that's departed in the last few hours. Checking reservations ... nothing ... nothing. And —*oh*. Here we go. Thomas Bartlett. Departing tomorrow morning. First flight on Southwest to Dallas. Probably going to connect from there, but I don't see another reservation."

"That's good enough," Winston said.

"Can you check the airport hotel?" Linda asked. "We know he's there right now, but the tracker can't narrow it down to a room."

"Hang on ... yeah," she said after a long pause

and the clicking of keys. "Room 512. I'd hack in and send you a key code, but that's above my pay grade. Want me to get Denny or Mario on it?"

"No," Winston said, hating the word. Denny Walker and Mario Lombard were probably the best hackers in the business, and he trusted them both completely. But this had to stay contained, and, dammit, he couldn't take the chance that they were too close with Seagrave.

"We'll handle it on this end," he said as Linda took the exit for the airport, then made the next quick turn toward the hotel.

The airport had been converted from a former Air Force base, and the main administration building had been repurposed as a hotel. The place was round, reminding Winston of a coliseum, and he hoped that wasn't a portent that they'd be on public display or end up locked in combat with the world looking on. They let the valet take the car, then hurried inside.

"Keep an eye out," Linda said as they headed toward the elevator bank. "He could be in the bar."

They saw no sign of him in the bar or the main open area, though, and as soon as they arrived at the fifth floor, they followed the curving perimeter toward Bartlett's room, passing a maid's cart on the way.

When they reached 512, Linda kept her weapon in one hand and pressed the forefinger of her other over the peephole before knocking. "Housekeeping," she called, her voice pitched so high Winston wasn't sure he'd have been able to identify her with his eyes closed.

Hopefully, neither would Tommy Bartlett.

He waited beside the door, his gun ready. Except the door never opened.

"Hiding or not in there?" Linda whispered.

"We'll find out." Winston answered with an equally low voice, before raising it. "Dammit, sweetheart, I asked if you had the key before we left the fucking room. If I have to go all the way down to the lobby because you were too empty-headed to—"

"No," she said, her voice shaky as she played along. "Baby, it's okay. I'll get us in. I saw a maid right back there."

She scurried that direction as Winston paced and scowled for anyone who might be watching on video. Hopefully Linda's acting skills would suffice. If not, he assumed her pickpocketing skills would fill the slack.

Apparently acting won out, as she returned with the maid. He could see that her eyes were red and damp when they approached the door, and she offered him a thin smile and an even thinner voice as she said, "See, honey. I told you we'd get back in."

He huffed, then waved toward the door. "Well, go on then."

The maid hurried to unlock the door, and as he pushed inside, Linda offered a flurry of thank-yous to the woman.

The door fell closed behind them with a definitive *click*.

"You make a very convincing asshole," she said, after they'd both swept the room and re-holstered their guns.

"Might be in the bar," Winston said. "We know he's in the hotel. Or at least we know the tracker is," he added.

"I was just thinking that," she said, then looked in the closet. "Empty."

"Bathroom." He brushed past her to check. Sure enough, the coat was hanging behind the door.

"Maybe he did go down to the bar," Linda said. "We could have missed him. Or he picked someone up, and he's in her room."

"Could be," Winston said as he stuck his hand in the jacket pocket. He grimaced, then pulled out the contents—the tracker and a piece of paper. He winced as he skimmed the scrawled words.

"He's back in the wind," he told Linda.

"Are you sure?"

He passed her the crumpled sheet of hotel stationery on which was written, *Fuck you.*

"Well, hell." She met his eyes, hers reflecting his own irritation. "At least he's got good penmanship."

He laughed, and the tension lifted. "It will serve him well in life."

"So what now?"

"Well, he won't be on that flight," Winston said. "Either he booked it before and now will skip it. Or he booked it after he found the tracker to throw us off. Either way, he won't be on that plane."

"I agree. What about another flight? You can ask Emma to take another look."

He gave a quick nod of agreement, then dialed again.

"Well, hello there," Emma said. "You two just can't get enough of me."

"Can you check again? He gave us the slip. Room's empty except for his coat and the tracking device."

"Clever boy."

"We thought you could take another look at the manifests," Linda said. "Maybe he really was hanging out in the airport waiting to grab a flight at the last minute. And if nothing turns up there, could you check the car rental records?"

"There are a lot of car rental companies," Emma said. "And if he's got an alias...."

"I know," Linda said. "And he might. But we might get lucky."

"We really appreciate it," Winston added.

"Hey, I've got nothing else to do tonight except have sex."

Beside him, Linda stifled a laugh.

"Tell Tony I'm making sure you two enjoy the buildup to the main event."

"I thought I wasn't supposed to tell Tony anything."

"You can tell him whatever you want. You know I trust you. But I'd rather you just tell him you're doing me a favor."

"You got it."

"Call us back when you know something. And, Emma," Winston said.

"Yeah?"

"I owe you."

"No, you don't. I've always got your back, remember?"

Winston was still smiling when they ended the call. He looked at Linda, her expression unreadable. "What's wrong?"

"I don't have that."

He shook his head slowly, not understanding.

"A close friend is like that. I've been paired with partners before, but being deep cover like I am, I haven't gotten close to anybody. Not since—"

He frowned. "Since? Did you lose someone? Did a partner get killed?"

She met his eyes, and he thought he saw them glisten with tears. "Winston, dammit, I was talking about you."

"Oh." It was as if she had reached out and squeezed his heart. He stepped closer and took her hand in his. For a moment, he simply looked at her, a low burning need growing in him. Then he lifted her hand to his mouth and gently kissed her fingertips.

"What are you doing?"

He flashed her half-smile. "I think you know what I'm doing."

"We shouldn't," she said, but she didn't pull her hand away.

"We didn't know each other back then. You said we couldn't possibly have been in love. Maybe you're right. I don't know. It felt real to me. *You* felt real to me."

"You didn't know me."

"Maybe. I don't know. But the attraction was real." He slid his arms around her waist and moved closer, relishing the simple fact that she didn't resist. "Or am I wrong?"

"No," she said, her voice breathy. "You weren't wrong but—"

He cut her off with a kiss. Long and deep and tasting of honey and her sweetness. He wanted to lose himself in that kiss. Wanted to go with her back into memory, back into their past. Wanted to use this one, sensational kiss to make all the hurt go away, and then strip her bare and slowly, sweetly, start all over again.

That's what he wanted, and from the way she responded to his kiss, he thought she wanted it, too. But then her hands moved to his shoulders, and she gently pushed him away. He opened his eyes to see her lovely face looking at him, but now there was sadness in her tear-filled eyes.

"I'm sorry," she said. "I'm more sorry that you can possibly imagine. But we shouldn't. You know we shouldn't."

He shook his head. "I don't know anything of the sort."

She offered him one sad smile. "Maybe not," she said softly. "But I do."

CHAPTER FIFTEEN

I dream of his hands.

Soft caresses on my cheek. Gentle strokes against my breasts. And the urgent claiming as his fingers thrust inside me, making my body clench around him.

I arch up, my body seeking more of him. But, of course, he's not there, and I open my eyes to the sad reality that he hasn't touched me at all, I've only been dreaming.

I sink back into the pillow, breathing hard, my body tingly and awake. I roll to the side, expecting to see him there, then realize that I'm still living half in Hades, and half in a dreamland. Of course he's not beside me.

His side—to my right—is still made except for the missing pillow he took with him to the room's small sofa. I'd offered to share the bed, but he'd turned me down. A long stare, a twitch in the muscle of his cheek, and then a shake of his head. "I'd better not," he'd said, and I'd tried to ignore the lump of disappointment that had settled in my gut.

Tried, but failed, and as he'd settled on the couch with the pillow and a spare blanket, I'd gone to bed with him anyway—in my thoughts, at least—as I had for so many nights after Hades.

Back then, he'd been with me every night. Telling me in dreams that he forgave me. That he understood what I'd done and why I'd done it.

We'd make love through the night, and then he'd leave by morning, abandoning me to the life I'd made, alone.

Those dreams—fantasies—had been my anchor in that first year. His touch, albeit imaginary, was what had gotten me through.

But now here I am with the real man. A man who pushed every single one of my sensual buttons the first time I glimpsed him, and that doesn't seem to have stopped even after all this time.

I'd shut him down earlier because I know sleeping with him would be a bad idea. We can't get back what we had because there's nothing real to grab onto. Nothing but lies to anchor us.

But now, as I close my eyes and slide my hand between my legs, I ask myself if it matters.

It does. Of course it does.

But for tonight, maybe I don't care about the past or the future. Maybe I just want the now.

Maybe I just want Winston.

I slide out of bed and walk in my tank top and panties to the couch. I expect him to be asleep, so I'm surprised to see him still fully dressed and propped on his side. He's wearing earphones as he watches a movie on his phone. I glance at the screen and recognize it right away — *To Catch a Thief*.

I can't help but smile. It was one of our favorite movies to watch together, curled up on the couch with a bowl of popcorn.

He must hear me, because he turns over, then frowns. He takes out the earphones, then puts them and his phone on the table as he sits up. "Are you okay?"

I don't answer, and I see concern flicker in his eyes. "Linda?"

He starts to stand, but I reach out and push him back. Then I move forward and straddle him. My eyes lock on his as I try to read his thoughts. As I pray he won't push me away.

"What is this?" he asks, as his fingertip brushes my lower lip.

"I don't know," I admit. "A one-off, maybe. We can't— we can't go back to the way we were. That's gone. And it was never real in the first place. A shadow built on a lie." I draw in a shaky breath. "But even so, we never got to say goodbye."

"So this is an ending?"

"I don't know," I tell him again. "All I know is that I want you inside me. Is that terrible? Would I just be using you?"

"Using each other," he says, brushing my lower lip. "I don't think it would be terrible at all."

My heart flutters and my skin heats with the glow of lust. "Winston," I say. "Please."

This time he presses that finger to my lips and shakes his head. Then he reaches down and pulls my tank top up. It comes off easily, and he tosses it aside. I'm not wearing a bra, and my nipples tighten more in response to his gaze than to the cool air.

I bite my lower lip, forcing myself not to beg him to touch me. I trust him to know what he's doing. After all, there was never a day when Winston's touch didn't make me feel amazing.

Now is no exception, and when he reaches out to cup my breast, his thumb brushing lightly over my nipple, I lean my head back and gasp from the sweet sensation of the electric heat slicing through my body, a straight shot from my nipple to my sex.

His mouth closes over my other breast, his teeth grazing my nipple. I slide my hands down his back, wanting to feel him, and I sigh in pleasure when my fingers slip beneath his untucked shirt to find the bare skin of his back.

He lifts his mouth from my breast, then kisses me. Softly at first, then harder and deeper, his tongue warring with mine as his hand slips down, lower and lower, until his fingers are inside my panties.

I whimper as he brushes my clit. "Take them off," I say, but he ignores me, instead teasing me with his fingers as his tongue does the same with my mouth. I want to make demands—deeper, harder—but I'm lost in a haze of sensuality. My body tightening. *Needing.* I want him inside him, and yet this is incredible. The intimacy of his mouth. The feel of his fingers. And—oh, God—the wild, crazed need that bursts over me as his fingers fill me.

"That's it, sugar. You're so damn wet. Do you have any idea how beautiful you are? How powerful it makes me feel to see you like this, wanting me? Demanding all the pleasure I can give you?"

"Yes," I murmur. It's the only word I can manage.

"Will you do something for me, baby?"

"Anything."

His fingers tease, and I grind against them, my clit rubbing his hand as his fingers thrust deeper.

"Come for me, darlin'. Come for me right now."

CHAPTER SIXTEEN

Winston moaned as Linda cried out, her body clenching around his fingers as if his words really had sent her over the top. He was so hard now it was painful. And it wasn't even that he'd gone so long without touching a woman.

No, it was *this* woman. Linda. The woman he'd once craved every moment of every day. The woman he'd mourned so damn deeply. And here she was alive and in his arms and it was as if he wanted to both celebrate her being here and punish her for leaving him in the first place.

She sighed, her body ceasing to tremble, and her eyes fluttering open. "I want more," she whispered. "Not just your fingers." She shifted position, leaning in to kiss him as she straddled his leg.

"No," he whispered.

She leaned back, and he saw the hesitation in her eyes.

He smiled, then flicked the band of the panties. "Take them off."

The corner of her mouth twitched, and she did as he ordered, then slid back on him, her hips undulating as she rubbed herself against the material of his slacks. "You?"

He shook his head. "No."

He could see that she expected him to say more, but right now, this was what he wanted. His wife, naked on his lap, his only mission to make her more and more desperate.

He cupped her bottom as she shifted, no longer straddling his leg, but his hips. His cock. He was so damn hard, and the motion of her body was making him harder, driving him a little insane. And not just her touch, but the fact that she so obviously wanted him. The years hadn't diminished the heat between them. If anything, it seemed more intense, a knife-edge added to it, giving this night a hint of danger along with the passion.

"I should spank your ass for leaving me," he said, not even sure where the words had come from. That had never been a thing with them.

"You probably should," she agreed, and he almost moaned aloud in pleased surprise. "For that matter, you should probably tie me to the bed again."

He leaned back to find her looking at him. Her eyes were on his, heavy-lidded with lust. But she was biting her lower lip, a sign he recognized from the past. Something she wanted in bed, but had been hesitant to tell him.

Interesting.

"Close your eyes," he said, and when she did, he smacked her on the rear. She gasped, but her eyes stayed closed—and she grinded against him even harder.

He slipped his hand between their bodies and thrust a single finger inside her, finding her even more wet and slippery. *Oh, dear God, she was going to break him.*

"I like this," he said. "Watching you. Seeing you like this. Your skin flushed and your lips swollen. So desperate you're willing to get yourself off while I watch."

"Willing?" Her brow rose. "That's part of what makes it so hot."

He grinned. "I can't argue with that." She was more bold now than she'd been in Hades. He probably wouldn't like the reasons if he thought about it too much, but he couldn't deny that he liked the results. Their lovemaking before had been on the sweet end of the spectrum. Wonderful, but tame.

This was raw and rough, and he craved it. Needed it. And the idea that she would agree—

hell, had suggested—to be bound ... well, he couldn't deny that he wanted that, too.

"Come on," he said, easing her off of him, then leading her to the bed. "Lie down."

She did, and he glanced around the room, finding the hotel robe tossed over a nearby chair. He pulled the sash free, then walked to where she was stretched out on the bed, her arms already above her head. There was no headboard, but he had her move so that her head was at the corner, her body diagonal across the king-size bed. He used a slipknot to bind her wrists, then tied the other end to the frame.

"Close your eyes," he said. "And keep them closed."

"Yes, sir," she said, with enough of a smirk that he knew they were both going to enjoy the game.

He peeled off his clothes, then sat beside her, wanting first to simply look at her. Once, he'd been so familiar with her body. Even now, he recognized the little things. The scar from an appendectomy. The birthmark on her pussy, visible only because she shaved. The curve of her neck. The tiny mole on her left breast.

He looked, then he used his finger to trace from point to point, making a game out of seeing if he could make her arch up or bite her lip as he worked his way down her body. It wasn't hard. She was so damn responsive.

"Tell me," he said, pulling his hands away and moving back so that his hip wasn't brushing her skin. "Tell me what you want."

"I want you to touch me. Please. Don't stop. Touch me, and then make love to me. Make me explode."

It was a demand too tempting to resist, and he circled the bed until he could take her ankles, then tug her legs apart. If he'd had more ties, he would have bound her that way, too, but all he could do was demand that she promised to keep her legs wide.

She nodded, and then bit her lip as he stroked his fingertip along the soft skin between her thigh and her sex. He let his gaze roam slowly over her. Her smooth skin. Her beautiful face. Her pussy, wet and ready for him. "You're so damn beautiful," he said.

"Please."

"Please what?"

"Untie me. I changed my mind. I want to touch you."

He grinned. "No."

She opened her eyes and he pointed at her. "No," he repeated. "You know the rules."

She closed her eyes, and he resumed touching her.

With every glance and stroke, the need built in him. The need to be inside her. To claim her. To take her like this, bound to the bed, a proposition that had become even more enticing since she'd asked to be released.

Slowly, he kissed his way up her inner thighs, enjoying the way she strained to keep her legs spread and struggled against the bonds at her wrists. He licked her clit with the tip of his tongue, satisfied when she arched up and cried out. Then he moved higher. Starting at her neck and kissing and licking his way down, enjoying both the taste of her and the way she responded to his touch.

He was teasing the soft skin of her mons when she started to beg again. "Please." She tugged against the cord holding her arms in place. "Please, I want you inside me. Winston, please."

He wanted to draw it out more. To make her desperation like a living thing. But how the hell could he when he was already so incredibly hard, his body so tense that he was about to explode right then.

"Please," she begged, and he had to give in, as much for himself as to satisfy her pleas.

He wanted to go slow—to tease both of them—but he couldn't. He was too hard and she was too ready, and he thrust inside her with one bold stroke, sinking deep and making her arch up and cry out, begging him to fuck her harder as he pistoned inside her, closer and closer until, finally, her core tightened around him, bringing him all the way over the edge.

They exploded together, the world falling in starbursts around them. And in that moment—that singular moment—he wasn't sure if they were in the past or the present or sometime in between.

All he knew for certain was that she was his. For tonight, at least, they were together.

Later, when she was untied and they were spooned together, he whispered, "Why?"

He couldn't see her face, but he heard the smile in her words when she said, "Because I knew it would be amazing."

She rolled over, facing him. "And it was."

"It was," he agreed. "And?"

She drew in a breath. "And I wanted you to know I trusted you. Completely. It's important for the mission."

"I did know that."

She shook her head. "You thought you knew. Now you really do."

For a moment, they simply held each other's gaze. Then she said. "This doesn't change anything. The past is gone, Winston. This was wonderful, but not important."

"I know," he said, but that was a lie. It *was* important. And he had a feeling it changed everything.

CHAPTER SEVENTEEN

H e was swimming naked in the quarry outside of Hades with Linda beside him, their bodies twined together, as slippery as eels. The sun beat down on them, and they laughed as the water buoyed them. He'd missed her so much, and now to have her in his arms again, to feel weightless with her the way he did now, it was as if he had suddenly been shown a small slice of heaven.

"Hey." Her soft voice filled his senses.

"Hey, yourself."

She smiled, the expression as bright as the sun above them. He tugged her closer, and they laid back, floating easily on the water, their fingers twined together as they looked up at the white, fluffy clouds. It was a perfect day. Absolutely perfect.

Nothing could go wrong. Nothing could take her from him, not again. He'd lost her once, but he'd

found her, and damned if he wasn't going to keep
her this time. Damned if he wouldn't die to make
sure that happened.

He shifted, the water splashing against him as
he turned his head to look better at her. "You know
the truth, don't you?"

"I don't know what you mean."

"I love you."

"You don't know me. And I don't know you."

"But you do. We do."

"You have to be smart, Winston. You have to
really think about these things. You have to know
that nothing is ever really what it seems. Haven't
you learned that by now?"

"But you are back," he said.

"I am," she said. "But for how long?"

He could barely hear her voice at the end,
because that's when the clanging started. The alarm
bells ringing out, filling the quarry, echoing against
the stone walls.

They filled the space and the sound was soon
joined by a cacophony of machine-gun fire. Beside
him, Linda screamed, and when he looked over, she
was gone, and the water was red, red, red, and all he
could do was scream and scream and scream...

"Winston!"

He felt the hands on him, shaking him. "Winston!"

He sat upright, his heart like a jackhammer in his chest, his ribs aching from the force of his fear.

"You were having a bad dream."

He exhaled loudly and scrubbed his hands over his face. "You think?"

"It's Emma," she passed him his phone. "I wouldn't normally have answered it, but you weren't waking up, and I saw who was calling."

"It's no problem." He put the phone to his ear. "Emma?"

"Good God, Starr, what the hell is going on?"

"Just give me a sec." He stumbled out of bed and toward the coffee maker. It was the single cup kind, and Linda hurried over, slipping on the hotel robe as she moved toward him.

"I'll make it," she whispered. "Go take the call."

He nodded, grabbed his slacks from the bedside where he'd left them last night, and tugged them on. When he was finally seated and felt somewhat human, he focused on Emma. "Okay, shoot," he said, then gratefully took the coffee that Linda handed him.

"Well, he wasn't on the flight he had booked. A no-show. And he's not got another reservation. Like I said before, he could be at the airport waiting to grab a plane at the last minute, but I doubt it. He knows you're tracking him, he's going to try to get as far away as possible. That makes me think that he skipped out during the night."

"I agree. Hang on, I should have had this on speaker." He put the phone on the table and tapped the button as Linda came over, her own paper cup of coffee in her hand.

"I figure he rented a car, right? But there's no car rental in his name. Not from the Austin airport, not from anywhere in Austin."

"So we're out of luck?" Linda said.

"Actually, no. And you're welcome. I've always told Winston I'm a genius. I'm about to prove it."

Winston grinned. "I will happily repeat that if you get us a solid lead. What do you think you have?"

"As far as I can tell, he didn't rent a car, but there are a number of rentals that could be aliases, assuming this guy doesn't have much imagination. For example, someone named Barry Thompson rented a Buick."

"Barry Thompson, Tommy Bartlett. It's close," Emma said.

"But not definitive," Winston added. "I'd like more before we go chasing a ghost. You got any more?"

"I do indeed." He could practically hear the grin in Emma's voice. "The car that Barry Thompson rented was from a rental place that uses GPS trackers on their vehicles. Most do these days, but not all are as easy to hack into the tracking system."

"This one was easy, I take it?"

"Fuck easy," Emma said. "I got in because of my amazing skillset, thank you very much."

"Where is he?" Linda asked.

"That Buick is now parked on a piece of land outside of Austin near some tiny little town called Thrall."

"And this is relevant why?" Winston pressed.

"Well, as it just so happens, if you poke through about a million layers of paperwork, which yours truly did—you're welcome—you learn that the property in Thrall is owned by a company called CLM Accounting."

"Owned by Bartlett?" Linda asked.

"No clue," Emma said. "I haven't had time to dig that far. But considering that Bartlett is an accountant, at the very least I figure—"

"That it's worth us heading that direction to check it out," Winston finished for her. "You're right."

"Worst case, we've lost nothing but time," Linda said.

"And in the meantime, I'll keep looking," Emma promised. "I'll let you know as soon as I can confirm the property's his, unless you slap some handcuffs on the man and confirm your own way first."

Winston glanced at Linda, who nodded. "All right," he said. "Good work. I owe you."

"That's what I'm here for. But call in. I want to know you're okay. And, guys, listen, I haven't told anyone here about what you're doing. But if it gets nasty, and you need help, you know that you can trust us here."

"I do." He glanced at Linda, then glanced away. "We'll keep that in mind." He ended the call, then looked at Linda again. "I do trust them," he said. "But I trusted you. I trusted Seagrave. And I'm not liking the way it feels when trust gets pulled out from under you like a cartoon carpet."

She moved to sit on the coffee table, so that she was right in front of him. She took his coffee away, then held his hands. "That was a long time ago, and I was undercover. You had secrets, too. And as for Seagrave, maybe you can still trust him. That's what we're trying to find out."

"This isn't a new thing," Winston said, realizing that was true even as he spoke the words. "It's this business. If you do undercover work, you hold a piece of yourself back. Always. It comes with the territory. But I never held back with you. Not anything that mattered."

"Nothing except who you really were," she said, her voice serious even though her expression was teasing.

"Not even that," he said. "You always had my

heart, Linda." He felt the sharp pang in his heart. "Did I have yours?"

"Yes," she whispered. "What we had was real— at least as real as it could be in a bubble of lies."

He nodded, wanting to argue that the lies didn't make the emotions any less real. But he understood what she meant, and right then they didn't have time.

"Thank you for last night," she said.

"Is it terrible for me to say that I don't mind that it took until morning for us to get a lead on Bartlett?"

Her smile was slow. "Under the circumstances, he's a man we really need to find. But no. I know exactly what you mean."

He leaned forward to kiss her, but she pressed a fingertip to his lips. "No. We need to go, and you know it."

"I do."

She pulled away from him. "Time to get dressed and go hunt an accountant."

"Here," Winston said, pointing to the tiny road hidden among the trees. "I think that's it."

Linda tapped the brakes and made the sharp turn onto the rutted dirt lane. Trees lined one side of the road, a field for grazing cattle on the other.

As far as Winston could tell, there was nothing but land ahead. He frowned, hoping they hadn't made a wrong turn on the spiderweb of tiny roads.

For a few silent minutes, the car bounced over the uneven surface. Linda grimaced. "How far?"

Winston checked his phone again. "The GPS is shit out here, but I think it's just another couple of miles."

"Well, it doesn't look like anyone's following us, so that's good. Of course it might also be that we're going to a house that has absolutely nothing to do with Tommy Bartlett. In which case it's a big old waste of time."

"I've spent a lot of time in small towns," Winston said. "If nothing else, maybe whoever we find in that house will have some nice warm cookies for us."

She laughed. "I think you have a very Norman Rockwell view of life these days."

"Or you're jaded."

"With what I've seen, of course I am. I'm surprised you aren't."

"Trust me, sweetheart, I am." He reached over and gently touched her shoulder. "But I'm starting to learn that sometimes things aren't as bad as they seem."

She turned her attention away from the choppy road to meet his eyes, hers shining with something that might be hope. "Yeah. I know what you mean.

I never thought—well, I never let myself think—that I'd ever see you again. Much less that you'd ever know the truth. Or that you could forgive me."

"I have," he said seriously. "I was broken after you died. And then you broke me some more when you came back. But I think I've been healed."

She laughed. "The healing powers of sex?"

"The universal miracle cure," he teased.

"That was only about five minutes ago. Are you sure you've been super glued together?"

"I've still got some cracks that need mending," he said. "But I know you did what you thought best. And I believe you did it because you loved me."

"I did."

"And I'm sorry that the man you made that sacrifice for wasn't the man you thought you knew."

He watched as she nodded slowly. "Well, we both owe each other an apology for that. And I think that neither one of us can judge each other for the secrets we kept back then."

"So here we are, moving forward, trying to extricate ourselves from the mess that lingers from the past."

"Not just the past," she said. "Look around. We're in the middle of some deep shit, and it's tied to Billy Hawthorne. And Billy's trying to build up a network using the scattered remnants of the Consortium."

"I know. And that's why we're out here in the middle of nowhere trying to find his accountant. More important, trying to find who on the inside is trading secrets with scum like Billy Hawthorne."

She nodded, and they drove silently for a while, both thinking about their respective bosses and the possibility that either was dirty.

At least Winston assumed she was thinking about that. God knows he was thinking about Seagrave. He'd known Seagrave for over a decade now, and he had trouble believing the man would steal a stapler from the SOC's supply room, much less national secrets.

"Collins is the one who pulled me out," she said, and though it sounded like a random statement, Winston knew it confirmed that her thoughts had been running along the same lines as his.

"Pulled you out?"

"Yeah. I told you I was recruited from one of those career fairs, and that's true. But what I didn't tell you was that I was having a very hard time of it before that. I was flat broke and seriously considering dropping out."

She shot him a sideways glance. "My childhood was a nightmare, so I was used to things being hard, and I was also used to doing whatever it took to get by. But I still wasn't managing. I'd worked shit jobs for minimum wage to get my GED, then barely managed to cover tuition. I got some aid, but not much, and right before the career fair, I was at the end of my rope. Money," she said, turning to look at him. "It drives people to do things they wouldn't normally do."

"If Seagrave or Collins really is dirty, it's because of a payday."

She nodded, then cleared her throat. "Anyway, I was working three jobs, I was exhausted, and I was coming close to failing all of my classes. I knew how to survive on the streets, because that's what I'd done after I ran away, and I started thinking that maybe the thing to do was quit my shitty waitress gig and just turn tricks."

He tensed, hating that she'd even had to consider that. "Had you done that when you ran away?" He kept his voice steady, though he dreaded the answer.

"No," she said. "But I had friends who did. So I figured it was an option. Either that or selling drugs, and that doesn't sit with me at all. My body is mine to sell, but dealing drugs?" She shook her head. "No. I'd seen the effects on the street. No way I was playing in that sandbox."

"I'm glad," he said. "And you didn't have to sell yourself, either, I assume. Because of Collins?"

"Yeah." She smiled with the memory. "I was talking with this girl I knew about doing the escort thing. Better than a streetwalker, right? At least the clientele knows how to wear a suit. We were chatting on the quad, and this guy followed me after I left to go work my shit. He told me to stop, that he wanted to talk. I almost told him to fuck off, but then I realized I'd seen him before."

"At the career fair."

She nodded. "He wasn't working the booth. He'd been hovering around. He asked if I recognized him, and I said I did. That's when he smiled and said *I thought you'd have the gift.*" She shrugged. "He meant I could make a good spy. Apparently, I pay attention to things."

Winston laughed. "As far as recruitment stories go, that's the best I've heard."

"Right? Well, anyway, he ended up being my mentor. I was so young that he was like a surrogate dad, too. So the bottom line is that I don't like what we're doing. I don't like the fact that I believe that it's possible. But here's the thing," she added, taking her eyes off the road to really look at him. "I know that it can. Because I've seen the dirty underbelly. And it's nastier than anyone on the outside can imagine."

"You're right," he said. "Neither one of us can ignore the possibility that a man we respect could be bad."

"No," she said. "We can't." She took one hand off the steering wheel and reached for him. He took her hand and squeezed, absurdly pleased that she'd reached out to him for the connection. "It's probably weird, and I wish that neither one of us was going through this, but since we are, I'm glad that we're going through it together."

He felt a warm rush of pleasure from her words. "Yeah," he said softly. "Me, too."

For a few minutes, they continued down the road in silence, the ride getting bumpier and bumpier as the surface got worse. Then Winston saw the small wooden mailbox in need of paint. And, if the GPS was right...

"There," he said, pointing. "Turn right here."

She did, then had to stop about ten yards down the dirt driveway when the path was blocked by a wood and barbed-wire gate.

"Hang on." He got out of the car, hoping it was meant to keep livestock in and not people out. Sure enough, it was easy to unfasten and push to the side. He did, and she drove through. He kept the gate open, just in case they needed to get out of there quickly, and hopped back in the car.

"Where's the house?" she asked peering down the dirt driveway.

"Over that rise, I assume." He made a forward motion with his hands. "Onward."

She put the car back in gear, and they moved slowly down the road, the dust swirling around the car as they did. Sure enough, as they crested the gentle rise, they saw a small clapboard house, not much more than a cabin, really. Boxy and tiny and, from the looks of it, empty.

Or maybe not empty, Winston thought as he caught sight of the forest green Buick parked behind a woodshed.

Linda's smile was broad as she said, "Got him."

"Back up a bit so the car's hidden by the rise. If we're lucky he hasn't heard us."

She did as he asked, and they took the long way around, scoping out the house as they moved, weapons drawn. But there was no movement in or outside the building.

He made a motion to indicate that he was going closer, and she moved to cover him. He crept to the back door, wondering if Bartlett was asleep in there. Or maybe out for a walk. Or maybe someone had met him here, and he'd left in another vehicle altogether. He hoped not. If that was the case, they could kiss Bartlett goodbye. At least for the short term. And finding him again, really would entail bringing in a full team from Stark Security.

He reached the backdoor without incident. Unlocked. He signaled to Linda, who stayed low as she hurried to his side. On three, he turned the lock, and they went in, him high and her low.

Silence.

The kitchen was empty, but he caught Linda's arm as she started toward the next room.

"Do you smell that?" he whispered.

She sniffed, then nodded. "Death."

Winston's stomach turned. She was right. It was the scent of blood drying in the heat.

With weapons drawn, they moved into the small living area, then into the even smaller bedroom.

Sure enough, Tommy Bartlett lay spread-eagled on the floor, face down in a pool of his own blood.

CHAPTER EIGHTEEN

"His hands," I whisper. "Oh, God. Did you see his hands?"

Winston nods, looking as queasy as I feel. They've been mutilated, the fingers and thumbs removed. And in this heat, the smell is horrific.

"The laptop." I swallow the bile that is rising in my throat. "Whoever killed him wanted to make sure that even dead he couldn't unlock that laptop."

"You're right." He turns to look directly at me. "It can be accessed by a retinal scan, too."

Oh, God, he's right. I don't want to, but I take a step closer to the body, putting me at his head. I kneel, then grab his hair so that I can pull his head up.

Immediately, I recoil, gagging at the sight of the empty sockets where his eyes used to be.

"They might still be nearby." Winston's voice is

urgent but gentle as he helps me to my feet. My legs are shaking, and I remind myself that I see death all the time. For that matter, had things not gone so completely off-kilter, I would probably have killed this man myself.

I grimace. The thought doesn't make me feel better. And God knows, I wouldn't have tortured him or mutilated his body.

"We need to look around. The eyes. They might still be useful."

I cringe, but nod. "I've seen a lot," I say. "But that, I don't know if—*shit!*"

The scream rips out of me as a bullet shatters the window and whizzes by my head to lodge in the wooden wall behind us. At the same time, Winston grabs my arm and yanks me to the ground.

"Let's go!" He has his weapon out and rises just enough to peer over the windowsill before dropping back to the floor. "The shooter must be hidden by the trees. I don't see anyone."

"Head to the back. We need to get to the car."

He nods, then urges me to follow him.

I hesitate, realizing something. "Go ahead," I tell him, then crawl back to the dead man and carefully pull out his wallet with two fingers at the edges. I grab a paper bag from Whataburger and shove the wallet inside, then I toss in a nearby magazine and soda can, both sitting on the end table nearest the body.

From the doorway into the kitchen, Winston urges me on. I stay low as I sprint to him. He's right, of course. Whoever fired at us was at the side of the house right then, but if he circles to the back before we get to the car...

"More than one?" I ask as we pause in the kitchen.

"I hope not."

I grimace. At least he's honest. "Give me the key," I say. "You cover me. I'll come get you."

I can tell he wants to protest.

"Just do it," I say. "I'm a kickass driver. And we don't have time to argue."

He gives me the key. "Go."

I do, sprinting out the door, my legs churning as my thumb punches the button on the remote to unlock the car. I keep expecting a bullet in my back, but there are none, and I make it all the way to the car, then slide in behind the wheel safe and sound.

Maybe there really is only one shooter, and he's on the far side of the house right now.

I say a silent thank you to the universe, then start the car. I hurry forward, maneuvering until I'm parallel to the back of the house so that Winston doesn't have far to run. It's not a long distance, and, since it was clear for me, I expect—hope—that it will be for him, too.

Of course it's not, and I've only moved a few

feet when a spray of bullets hits my side, shattering the driver's side window and coming close enough that the buzz of the bullet fills my ear.

"*Shit.*" I accelerate with my head as low as possible, then swing around in front of the door as Winston races toward me. A moment later, the back passenger door flies open, and Winston dives in.

"*Go!*" he shouts. "Just go!"

I do, the gas pedal all the way to the floor.

We skid on the uneven surface but soon get traction, and we go bouncing toward the main road, the back passenger door hanging open as Texas dust fills the car.

"At least two," he says, shifting in the back seat and yanking the car door closed. Then he crawls into the front and straps himself in beside me.

"Get us the hell out of here."

"That's the plan," I say. "We need to lose them, but this isn't exactly the vehicle for that. Our best hope is that it takes them a while to get to wherever they hid their car."

He turns and looks behind us. "Yeah, you're not going to be getting that wish."

I glance in the rearview mirror to see a BMW eating up the distance between us.

Shit.

Not only was I hoping for more time, I would

have preferred our enemy not to be in a vehicle that could run circles around this one.

"We need to get to the open road," I say. "I'll out-maneuver these fuckers."

How I'm going to do that on straight, shoulderless, country roads is something I'm not thinking about at the moment. The eternal optimist. That's me.

"Yeah?" His voice is tight. "Well, until then, we have a problem."

I'd been concentrating on the surface of the drive, but he's looking further ahead. I follow his gaze to see that the gate we'd left open is now closed. Not to mention locked with a chain.

"Oh, for fuck's sake." I fervently wish for manual transmission, but instead try to press the gas even harder. "Hold on," I say, then maneuver the car so that the point of impact is right where the gate latches to the frame. We collide at full speed, and while the chain doesn't break, the post comes out of the ground, and we're able to bounce right over the barbed wire gate. I wince, expecting the tires to blow out, but we get lucky, and they don't. Maybe whoever's following us won't be as lucky.

That theory is negated seconds later when the Beemer careens over the barbed wire, makes a wild turn onto the road, and roars toward us. And to make matters worse, someone leans out of the passenger side and fires, shattering our back window.

Winston and I both duck. "Any brilliant ideas?" I ask.

"Lose them."

"Great. Glad you thought of that."

I don't take my eyes off the road to look at him, but I'm positive he's sending me a sarcastic look. "Just thinking out loud."

"No. I appreciate it. Anything you can think of to get us out of here works for me."

"And you? Any ideas?"

"Other than just driving like a bat out of hell? Not really."

Even as I say the words, though, I see a flatbed loaded with baled hay coming toward us from the opposite direction.

"This will work."

"Whoa," Winston says. "What the hell are you thinking?"

"Quiet. I need to concentrate."

He makes a low noise in his throat, but to his credit, says nothing. He does, however, brace himself with the dashboard and door handle. *Smart man.*

"Just warn me when you—"

His words are cut off as I make a hard U-turn in front of the flatbed, so close the driver has to slam on the brakes, and we come within mere inches of

missing it as I skid off the road, then frantically try
to accelerate on the soft shoulder to get ahead of
the now-slow truck.

By some miracle, I manage that, and now I aim
the Toyota straight ahead, so that we'll pass the
BMW heading west while we go east.

As I'd hoped, the BMW driver doesn't fire—not
with witnesses. And it also can't turn around to
follow us, because it's now even with the truck, and
has no clearance for a U-turn until it's past the
flatbed.

It's not a lot of time, but we can make it work,
and once again, I put the Toyota to the test, flooring
it and making the first turn I see, then another and
another until we're lost in a web of ranch roads,
county roads, and private drives.

Finally, I pull over behind a whitewashed
Baptist church. The parking lot is empty, and as
soon as the engine dies, I lean back in the seat,
breathing hard.

My heart is still pounding when I feel his hand
take mine. I look over to find him grinning like a
fiend. "What?"

"That was some damned impressive driving. I
thought we were going to buy it in front of that
truck."

"I haven't had to do something like that in a
very long time."

We grin at each other, both breathing hard, and

right then, all I want to do is kiss him. I don't—
crazed killers in a BMW could turn up at any
moment. But I definitely bank the thought as a
future plan.

I start the car, put it in gear, and pull out onto
the road. "Where to?"

"Back toward Austin for now," he says. "We
need to find a place to hole up, and then figure out
if there's a way to break into that damn laptop
without the biometrics."

"Actually," I say, "we need to pool our
resources and see if either of us has a contact who
can manufacture fake biometrics. Or a fingerprint,
anyway."

For a moment, he just stares at me. "Wallet,
can, magazine. You were gathering fingerprints."

I nod, pleased with myself for thinking of it,
and with him for being up to speed.

"Excellent. You drive. I'll call Noah."

"Noah?"

"Tech genius. He's how I listened in on your
conversation with Bartlett."

"You trust him?"

"I do. But, full disclosure. He's done some work
with the SOC."

I draw in a breath, knowing that a smarter
agent would say no. Because there is no way to
guarantee this guy is safe. But maybe I'm not as
smart as I used to be, because I nod and tell

Winston that if he trusts Noah to keep it to himself, then I'm okay with him calling.

Besides, it's not as if we have other options.

"Fast food," I say.

"What?"

"We'll meet him in a parking lot," I clarify. "Whoever's looking for us won't expect to find us there, and if they do find us, we'll be close enough to a highway or at least a major road to make serious tracks. Plus, I'm hungry."

"Good plan."

"And I think you should ask Noah to bring a car for us. He can either call an Uber to get back or he could take this car. I think he'd be better off with the ride share, though."

"Agreed."

Soon enough, Winston maps the way to a nearby McDonald's, and we're heading that direction. He texts Noah as well, who replies that he'll meet us there soon. Since we're out in the country, and he's still in the city, we beat him to the restaurant. We order from the drive through, then head to the back of the parking lot where we wait, me fidgety in my seat.

"Have you noticed that neither Seagrave nor Collins has called to check in with us?" I ask.

"What are you saying?"

I shrug. "I'm not sure, really. Just that we haven't updated either of them after Bartlett's supposed no-show. Shouldn't each of them be wondering if they have an agent down?"

He studies my face, then reaches for one of my French fries since he's already finished his order. After a moment, he nods. "They both trust us to do the job, so it could be that they're leaving us alone to do it. It could also be that they know that we're onto them. Whichever one of them is bad." He meets my eyes. "Or both of them, working together."

"That's a horrible thought," I say. Beside me, he nods. Then he reaches across the car and holds my hand. That simple touch sends shocks running through my body, and I wish we were alone in a room, naked and wild and able to burn off some of this frantic fear and energy.

"You're not alone," Winston says, and for a moment I think he's talking about my sexual fantasies. "We're in this together."

"Right." I hope I'm not blushing. I'm debating the wisdom of kissing him when his phone dings, signaling that Noah has entered the parking lot.

At Winston's nod, I flash the lights. He's brought us a Land Rover, and he pulls into the space beside us, then moves into the Toyota's back seat, frowning at the scattered glass.

"Just a day in the life," Winston says, and we all laugh.

After the introductions and the summary of

what our problem is, Noah nods reassuringly. "Assuming I can get good fingerprints, I should be able to get access. If not, I can try to hack the laptop."

"No," I say firmly. I meet Winston's eyes, and he clears his throat.

"Sorry. We weren't clear. You're not getting the laptop at all."

"It's not that we don't trust you," I say, "although to be honest, I don't even know you. It's just that if anything happens to the information on that laptop, we're really and truly screwed. It stays with us."

Winston hesitates, then nods. "If it turns out that you need to search the laptop for a clean print, we'll make more arrangements. But see if you can manage from what we've given you."

Noah nods, looking into the Whataburger bag. "I should be able to tell if I can pull an acceptable print within the next few hours. If you don't hear from me, then everything's good."

"And after that, how long will it take you to make a finger we can use?"

"Minimum of two days."

"That long?"

He chuckles. "This isn't an episode of the latest spy drama. I can't scan a print into the computer and have it spit out a latex thumb that will give you access. I can do this—maybe—but it's going to take some time."

I nod.

"And without the laptop I can't even test it, so we may have to repeat the process all over again after the first time."

Winston looks at me, and I shake my head again. I want this over. I want to know if the man I trusted my entire life adult life is dirty. And in order to know that for certain, I can't risk whatever information is on that computer. And that means it stays with us.

"Then I guess we'll have to start over if it comes to that," Winston says.

Noah nods. "Fair enough. Here are the keys to the Land Rover," he says, passing them to Winston. "Where can I reach you? This number?"

Winston shakes his head. "No. We're going to ditch these cell phones and get new ones. Burners." I look at him, because that's not something we've discussed yet, but I agree, and nod.

"All right then, you contact me. Do you have a safe location where you can wait until the print is ready?"

"No," I start to say, but Winston speaks over me.

"Yes," he says. "We've got somewhere to go."

CHAPTER NINETEEN

"Wait," I say as he maneuvers the Land Rover through downtown Llano, Texas. Which, to be fair, consists of a courthouse on the square and the few retail shops and restaurants that surround it. And, of course, The Marquis, the movie theater that his parents own.

"Wait? For what?"

It's a fair question. Traffic this afternoon consists of maybe five cars. It's a darling town, but a sleepy one.

"Just pull over a second," I say when he looks at me in question.

To his credit, he doesn't argue, just pulls into a parking space in front of an ice cream store. "I adore your parents, really I do. And I want to see them again, even though it's going to be really weird. But are you sure this is a good idea? I mean aren't we putting them in danger? Surely, Seagrave will look for you there."

"It's a good point, but no. Exactly because he knows me well."

I lift my hands in a sign of general confusion.

"He knows that I'd never in a million years put my parents in danger. Which means he knows I would never hide out there."

I frown, turning that over in my head. And I have to admit, it's deviously clever. "And you're certain."

"Of course I am. Do you think I'd come here if I wasn't?"

"All right. I'll concede that Seagrave won't look here. But what about somebody else? What if it's Collins? He or Hawthorne search for Winston Starr, track down your family, and there you go."

He clears his throat, the tips of his ears turning slightly red.

I lift a brow. "Winston?"

"Yeah, well, there's something else I need to tell you."

I shift in the seat to look more directly at him. "All right. You have my attention."

"My last name isn't really Starr."

"Oh." That one genuinely surprises me. Especially since I have a marriage certificate with that name on it. "What is it?"

"It's complicated."

"I'm a good listener and reasonably clever. Try me."

He grimaces, but complies. "I applied to be an FBI agent right out of college. I was actually at Quantico when I got recruited into the SOC. And, I don't know. Maybe I'd seen too many movies, but when they described the kinds of missions I could expect, I started to worry. Not about me, but about my family."

"Good God," I say. "What kind of insane recruitment films do they show over at the SOC?"

"It was all my imagination, but it was vivid. I had visions of me hanging by my toenails, finally managing to get free only to find out that my parents were in a cage in the basement, and the only way I could save them was if I shared state secrets."

I smirk, genuinely amused. But I also understand. "So you changed your name?"

"That was one of my prerequisites to agreeing to sign on with the SOC," he says. "I told the recruiting officer that I wanted to make sure my parents wouldn't get drawn in if I was tortured. I think he was just amused enough to agree to my demand."

I nod, fascinated.

"He helped me set up an essentially unbreakable alias. My brother had always teased me calling me too noble for my own good, and so I started going by the last name of Noble."

"I thought your middle name was Noble."

He shrugs. "I took on Starr for the Hades mission. When we got married, I wanted you to at least have heard the name I'd chosen for myself, so I told you it was my middle name. And now—well, now I mostly go by Starr, anyway. I wanted to keep it after ... well, just after."

"After me," I say softly.

He nods, and I feel that little twinge in my heart.

"On paper, I'm Winston Noble. But my friends know me as Starr."

"Sounds confusing."

He smiles. "It's really not."

"Well, it explains a lot. After you left Orange County I couldn't find you anymore."

"You looked for me?"

"I did."

Our eyes meet and hold for a moment until I glance away. I clear my throat. "But what's your actual birth last name?"

"Kellogg," he says.

"I like it. It's a nice strong name. But I like Noble and Starr better." I frown as something else occurs to me. "What about your parents. Do they know about the name?"

He shrugs. "I just played it up to paranoia in

law enforcement. They watch a lot of movies. Wasn't hard to make the case that the point of my alias was to protect my family from bad guys." He glances at me. "To be honest, I think my dad suspects my law enforcement career goes beyond the Sheriff's Department. But he's cool enough not to have ever asked."

I nod thoughtfully, thinking about what it must be like to grow up in a family of people who love you and respect your choices.

His hand moves to put the car back into gear, but I reach out, stopping him. "Hang on a second," I say. "If your name isn't Starr, then were we even married?"

"Yes," he says firmly. "That was the first thing I looked into before I asked you, actually. I wanted to make sure it was real. Turns out a marriage under a fake name is absolutely legitimate, although I probably should have fined myself for lying on a marriage license application. Apparently that's a misdemeanor."

I burst out laughing. "Well, I'm glad it wasn't a felony, I would have hated to have to bail you out for that."

He reaches over and squeezes my hand. "I know you don't think it was real. That our secrets somehow erase what we felt."

I press my lips together and look down at my lap, saying nothing.

"But if you could have felt the pain that swallowed me after seeing that burned out shell of a car and believing you were dead..."

He trails off, his voice breaking. "Well," he continues after a moment, "you'd know that not only did I really love you, but that it was as real a marriage as ever was."

"And you still feel that way? Even knowing the truth?"

He meets my eyes. "That our marriage was real? Yes. That your death broke me into pieces? Absolutely. I loved you, Linda. Christ, I loved you so much."

My mouth is dry and I swallow so that I can speak past the lump in my throat. "I'm not saying that our emotions weren't real. All I'm saying is that nothing else was."

"Well, maybe you're right and maybe you're not. I only know what I felt."

Felt.

The word hangs there, past tense. Not *feels.* Not now.

It shouldn't bother me—especially since I'm the one who's said that everything we had in the past was built on shadows. But it does. It bothers me more than I want it to.

I sit up straighter, shaking off the emotion. "We should go," I say. "Your parents will think we got lost."

"They're going to love seeing you again."

"Well, about that, the feeling is completely mutual."

"Linda!" Miriam Kellogg pulls me into her arms and hugs me tight. Just when I think my ribs are about to break, she pushes back, then looks me up and down. "You look fine. Does it hurt? Are you okay?"

"Mom," Winston says from behind me. "She's fine physically, unless you broke her with that hug. It was her memory that was broken."

"And I have it back," I say with extra cheer to hide the guilt of our lie. "I'm all better now."

She makes a clucking noise. "I can't believe it. Amnesia. I thought things like that only happened in the movies."

"Everything that happens in the movies probably happened in real life somewhere," a deeper voice says from behind me. I turn to find myself swept up in a giant bear hug from Dale, Winston's father. Like his wife, he ends the hug by pushing me back, his hands on my shoulders as he looks me up and down. "My God, girl, you are a sight for sore eyes. We've missed you."

"I've missed you too," I grin. "Or, I have since I remembered you." I shoot a sideways glance at

Winston, wondering if maybe this wasn't such a great idea.

He takes my hand. "We're glad to be here," he says. "It's been too long since I've seen either of you."

"Isn't that the truth?" Miriam says. "I'm so sorry that Richie and Nancy aren't here. Nancy's sister just had her third baby, so they went up to Tulsa."

"Well, we'll see them next time," I say, adding a note of sadness into my voice. In reality, I adore both Richie and Nancy, but I think that navigating between Dale and Miriam for the few days we'll be here is going to be challenge enough."

"Come on with me, son," Dale says. "Let the girls talk."

I feel a wave of panic, but Winston shoots me a smile as he follows his father, and I cling to it like a life preserver.

"I made cookies," Miriam says. "I used that recipe you sent me. Do you remember? The extra-chocolatey chocolate chip cookies?"

I sift through my memories, trying to pull up those moments of domesticity. It's not actually in my nature to be in the kitchen, and I faked it a lot.

Those cookies, however, I do remember. I'd gotten the recipe from a neighbor, and passed it to Miriam for bonus in-law points. "Even with amnesia, I don't think I could forget those."

She laughs, then passes me an oven mitt. I pull out the tray, then start to salivate at the rich choco-latey smell.

"Just put them on the cooling rack over there," she says. "Do you still take your coffee black?"

I nod, then sit where she indicates at the wooden kitchen table. She brings two cups over and takes the chair next to me. "I'm sure this must be strange. Such a long time has passed. Can you talk about what happened?"

"Well, you know that Winston was working on a case as sheriff."

He and I had talked about this in the car, the mix of truth and lies that we would tell them to justify the fact that I disappeared for years. They know that he was the sheriff, but they still have no idea about his intelligence work. And as far as they're concerned, I was exactly what I seemed to be to Winston, a low-level government employee who married the sheriff and made a home.

"Of course, we knew about that. Imagine, all that corruption in a town like Hades. I'm so glad that he left that place after you—well, after that car bomb."

I nod. "Apparently those people were trying to get him off the case. And to do that, they decided to target what was important to him."

"You. You were the most important thing in the world to him." She smiles wistfully "I remember your wedding. I've never seen that boy look so happy. And the letters he wrote. He talked about you all the time in those letters."

"Letters?" Winston used to write me a letter at every holiday, and I always thought it was such a sweet thing to do. I wish I still had them, but of course when one is fake-killed in a car bomb, one can't pack their belongings ahead of time. Leaving those letters behind is one of my biggest regrets.

"Yes. It was a habit that started back when he was young. Something I trained both the boys to do. It's a sad world we live in now with nothing but emails and texts. Who's going to find an old shoebox in the attic fifty years from now with treasured correspondence? Nobody, that's who."

I can't argue, because I don't disagree.

"But we got off topic," she says. "What happened in Hades?"

"Honestly, you know about as much as I do. They decided to target me, and then they bombed my car. They extracted two of my teeth. But they didn't kill me. I don't know why. And I don't know why my memories disappeared."

"And you woke up in Montana all these years later?"

I laugh. "I think maybe the first hint that something wasn't right was the fact that I couldn't stand the cold." It's a stupid joke, and she doesn't laugh. I don't blame her.

"Seriously," I say. "I was working in a library and I started having these flashes. So I went to a psychiatrist, and it took a couple of years. But we got my memories back. And then, although it was terrifying, I sought out Winston."

Miriam leans over and takes my hands. "You two had a special relationship. You still do. I know it must be very strange after all this time, but what you have is worth working for."

I swallow, my throat suddenly too thick. "Would you mind if we changed the subject? It's just so..."

She takes my hand and squeezes it. "Don't you worry, honey. I understand. And it's about time we take a plate of cookies in to the men. Don't you think?"

"Yes. That sounds like a wonderful idea."

We both stand, and I go automatically to the cabinet beside the window where the cookie platter is. When I pull it down, I see her looking at me, a teary-eyed smile on her face.

"I had a dream that one day you'd come back. I didn't think it could ever come true, because well, you were dead. It's nice to know that some things work out for the best."

"I think so too, Miriam."

She takes the platter from me and urges me over. "Now, I promised Dale I wouldn't ask this, but I'm going to anyway. You two are getting a late start, but before the, well, *accident*, you were talking about a family. Maybe there's still a chance for little Michelle?"

"*Mom!*"

We both turn, and even I feel guilty when I see the storm on Winston's face. He leaves the doorway and comes to my side, his arm going around my waist. I lean against him, fitting perfectly, the pain of those memories soothed by his touch.

"I'm sorry," Miriam says, looking between both of us. "I shouldn't have said anything about that. I know it's too soon. I just—"

"Really, Miriam, it's okay." I mean the words. I really do, but I'm grateful when Winston steers me out of the room. "We're going to unpack," he tells his mom.

"I'm sorry," he says once we're in his old bedroom, with the door closed behind us. "She's just deep in the grandparent zone."

"I know. It's okay. Really."

He nods, still looking frustrated. Then he draws in a breath. "Dammit, I know I should drop it. But now I have to ask."

"Ask what?"

"You used Michelle as your alias. Michelle Moon. The last name I understand—hell, I even like it, despite the gun-for-hire part."

I roll my eyes, but he continues.

"You were the moon to my Starr, right? But what should I think about Michelle?"

I close my eyes, then nod. "I know. I didn't mean for it to hurt you. Hell, I never thought you'd hear it."

Right before I had to leave, he and I had been planning our family. And although I wasn't pregnant yet, we were trying. And we'd decided that if we had a little girl, we would name her Michelle.

"I don't know why I decided to use it," I say. "Except maybe, maybe it was something I didn't want to give up."

I meet his eyes as I speak, but as soon as the words leave me, I look away.

"Well, then. Okay." He clears his throat. "And I am sorry if Mom made you uncomfortable."

"No, really. It's fine. She's happy I'm back. She wants the family to be all healed."

He looks at me. "The family."

I glance down at the floor. "That's what she wants."

"You're probably right," he says. He moves to sit on the edge of the bed. "And what is the status with the family?"

It's subtle, but I hear the edge in his voice.

"You're asking me big questions," I tell him.

"I want what we had," he says. "There. I'm laying it on the table."

"Except you can't have it," I counter. "I'm not the wife who makes cookies and has a garden."

He laughs, surprising me.

"What?"

"You had a garden. I felt sorry for those vegetables."

Despite myself, I laugh, too. "Okay, so that part of me you do know." We share a grin before I look down. "Seriously, I'm not a homemaker. And you aren't just a sheriff in a small town."

"And I'm saying none of that matters. That external stuff doesn't change the internal. Lots of people can't tell their spouse the details of their jobs. Some spouses don't want them to. They still love each other."

"Don't," I say. "Please. Don't you get it? I had Nirvana with you. What if we try again and it all falls apart? Then I lose those memories, too."

"You're scared."

"Of course I'm scared."

"I get it," he says, as he comes closer and takes my hands in his. "But you need to understand."

"Understand what?"

"That we're explorers, you and I."

"Are we?" My head's tilted to the side as I study his face. I have no idea where he's going with this.

"We're in uncharted territory here, darlin'. We'll just have to take it day by day."

"Yeah," I say. "Day by day."

"Inch by inch." He releases one hand so that he can trace his finger down my neck, then slowly toward the swell of my breast. "Tell me this, at least," he murmurs. "Are you still attracted to me?"

"Don't ask stupid questions."

His eyes light with his smile. "Then kiss me, and we can see about doing a little bit of that exploring right now."

CHAPTER TWENTY

I sip coffee on the front porch swing the next morning and watch the world go by as I remember the way Winston touched me last night. Sweet at first, and then with a wild urgency, as if he had to claim every part of me. Had to mark me as his.

Am I, though? Am I the woman he was making love to, or was he in bed with a memory?

I don't know the answer, and I push the thoughts away, wanting to enjoy the morning. A kid on a bicycle throws papers into the yards that line the street, and I can't help but feel as if I've been transported back to a different world. Hades hadn't been much bigger than this town, but it had never felt slow to me, probably because I lived in that dark place beneath the surface of the town. I saw the gears that moved that world and knew that everything up above was little more than a facade.

Here, though, life feels real. People walk by and they wave and smile. They pick the newspaper off their front stoop and then they actually read it, possibly going the entire morning without checking their phone.

What a crazy idea.

I put my cup aside and push the swing lightly with my toes as an elderly couple walks arm-in-arm down the sidewalk in front of the house. The man moves slowly as he helps his wife, and I get a lump in my throat watching them.

"I used to think that would be us."

I turn, the smile blooming on my face as I see Winston in the doorway. "Although I always assumed you'd be helping me along."

I scoot over so that he can join me on the swing. "In my fantasy, we never aged," I admit. I look back at the couple. "It was selfish of me. I never thought about what would happen when the work ended. I just wanted to be with you."

He takes my hand and we twine our fingers together. "Then I was selfish, too. I didn't tell you the truth, either."

I twist to look at him. "Would you have? If I hadn't—well, if it hadn't all fallen apart so quickly? Would we have told each other our secrets?"

"I think so. When it was over, why wouldn't we have?"

"Because we weren't who we said we were. And I—"

"What?"

"I would have been so scared of losing you," I admit. "I don't know, Winston. I honestly don't. I might have kept on lying. And I hate myself for that, because in the end, it would have poisoned everything."

"But it didn't happen."

I have to laugh. "No, instead this did. Not exactly the better alternative, you finding out I'm alive like that. And thinking I'm an assassin for hire."

"Oh, I don't know, darlin'," he says, laying his drawl on thick. "We're here now, aren't we?"

"Yeah," I say, a bit amazed that he's not still furious with me. I'd seen the rage in his eyes back in that hotel room. More important, I knew that I'd deserved it. He'd lied, too—that's true enough. But I'd left him broken, believing I was dead. And while I would do it again to keep him alive, I can't fault his fury. As far as I'm concerned, it's a miracle he doesn't hate me now.

I lean over and kiss his cheek, then watch his face light up. "What was that for?"

I shrug. "Does it have to be for anything?"

He shakes his head. "An unsolicited kiss with

no strings attached." He narrows his eyes as a
playful grin dances at the corner of his mouth.
"Protest all you want, sugar, but that sounds to me
like the start of something real."

"Winston..."

He lifts his hands in a gesture of surrender,
then pushes off of the swing. "I called Noah this
morning. Gave him my new cell number," he adds,
referring to the burner phones we'd picked up in a
Walmart on the way to Winston's parents' house.
"He said things were progressing nicely, but it was
going to take an extra day, maybe two."

"Oh," I say.

"I told him to take the time he needs. Can't risk
that laptop frying itself. I hope that's not a problem." His eyes lock on mine as he speaks. "It's a
small town, true. But surely we can find some way
to pass the time."

"It's no problem," I say, hoping he can't hear
the way my heart has started to flutter with the
pleasure of knowing that, at the very least, we'll
have an extra day together.

His grin is smug as he says, "I'm very glad to
hear it." He pulls open the screen door and starts to
step inside. "By the way, Mom's making banana
pancakes. Should be ready soon."

"Those are my favorite."

"I know," he says, then winks. "Why do you
think I asked her to make them?"

He steps inside, letting the door slam shut before I can respond. I consider following, but decide to stay, and I swing gently as I finish my now-cold coffee, a pleased smile lingering on my lips as I try very hard not to think about what might be.

There's something wonderfully settling about spending a lazy afternoon helping Miriam in the garden or watching Dale and Winston switch out the battery on Dale's ancient Chevy truck. And I'm completely fascinated by the catalogs of old movies that Dale has scattered around the living room.

He flips open a catalog to show me. "See? I use these to decide what to order for the theater. Each page has the basics about the movie, plus all the information on how I can go about getting it for my theater. But it's this here that I love the best." He taps the page. "These tidbits about the movies they add. Little bits of history to keep you intrigued."

He turns the catalog so I can see it better. "Who wouldn't want to know about Humphrey Bogart? Or Cary Grant?"

"I can't even imagine such a person," I say honestly.

He chuckles. "That's why we love you."

It's a casual statement to him, but it completely

ricochets through me, and I have to work to keep my smile light and my eyes dry. "So what are you going to show next?"

"You're in trouble now," Winston says as he comes from the kitchen to join us. He slides his arm casually around my waist, and I lean into him without even thinking about it. "He's going to suck you into the whole decision-making process."

"What do you think I was hoping for?"

"That's our girl," Dale says, and I have to swallow the lump in my throat. Because I've never had this. No close-knit family. No crazy chatter over the dinner table. No lazy afternoons sprawled in the living room with people you love.

When I was young, I'd had no family to sprawl with. And even when Winston and I were in Hades, it was just the two of us. We'd fantasized about a family—about our Michelle and her even more imaginary baby brother—but fantasies aren't the same. And while we'd come out here once in a while to visit, Hades is a long way from Llano.

At least, that was what Winston always said when his parents or Richie called to invite us out. Now I realize that part of his reticence was the need to keep secrets from them. And, probably, the fact that he had a job to do in Hades that went a lot deeper than his day job, just the same as me.

This isn't a vacation; I know that, of course. But I can't deny how much I love this bit of familial time. And I'm secretly glad that Noah's work on the biometrics is taking longer than planned.

By the time Miriam and Winston get tonight's dinner on the table, Dale and I have picked out the next few months of films for his little theater. "We can't do much about when we get to Christmas," he tells me. He holds up the catalog, showing one page bookmarked on *It's A Wonderful Life*, another on *Christmas in Connecticut*, and the third on *Die Hard*. I laugh. "I like the way you think, sir."

"How many times have I told you? Call me Dad."

"Thanks, Dad." I give him a smile and a quick kiss on the cheek, and when I turn around, I see Winston leaning against the doorframe, an odd expression on his face.

I walk to him and put my arms around his waist. "What?" He shakes his head, then bends to kiss me. I feel a twinge of guilt, because I know how disappointed his parents will be later when they learn that we're not together, especially since we can't tell them the reason behind our years-long ruse in the first place.

Right now, though…?

Well, right now, I don't care about what will happen later. For tonight, at least, I just want this moment, this man, and this family.

CHAPTER TWENTY-ONE

Winston woke slowly, his body spooned against Linda's, his face buried in her hair. It smelled like strawberries from the shampoo his mother kept in the guest bathroom, and he breathed it in, enjoying the intimacy of this moment.

Slowly, he traced his fingertip over her bare shoulder and down her arm, part of him wanting to rouse her, and the other part wanting to simply watch her sleep. The early morning light drifted through the curtains, and there was something so sweet and familiar about this moment, as if all the horror of the last few years had floated out to sea, gone and forgotten.

Ironic, since just a few days ago he'd raged at her, infuriated by the fraud he believed she'd perpetrated on him. But now he knew the truth—

she'd been trapped in a horrible situation, possibly even more horrible than what he'd endured. At least he'd been allowed to mourn. She'd had to live with the truth every single day. With the knowledge that he was out there, and yet they couldn't be together.

So many days had passed since Hades. But somehow, now that they were back together, it felt as if they had never been apart. She kept telling him that they were different people—that they never really knew each other—but that wasn't something he believed. He knew her heart, and she'd known his.

Now, he wanted to make this work.

Gently, he brushed a lock of hair off her face, careful not to wake her. She sighed, then rolled over in her sleep, her lips parted, her expression so soft. So innocent.

He smiled at the thought, because there was nothing innocent about what she'd done with that mouth last night. The way she traced kisses down his chest and abs. The way she'd taken his cock in her mouth, her attention on him so intense that he'd groaned aloud, then pulled a pillow over his face when she didn't relent, because he knew that at any moment he'd cry out with pleasure, shaking the damn walls and definitely waking his parents.

When she was done and he was spent, she'd eased up his body to lay on top of him, warm and naked and oh-so tempting. He'd kissed her and stroked her back, his hands cupping her ass as she wiggled teased.

"That was just for you," she'd protested when he tried to flip her over. "Just because I wanted to."

His heart had flipped at the mix of sultry and sweet in her voice, and he'd closed his eyes, wanting to ask her what this meant for them, hoping that it was more than just the pleasure of the moment.

But before he could broach the question, she'd slid down his body again, then looked up at him with that impish grin. Then she'd taken him into her mouth once again, and all coherent thought had left him, except for a lingering hope that they were back where they were supposed to be. And the fear that to her this was a deep dive into their past, and not a bridge to their future.

Now, he was tempted to wake her up and tell her that it was her turn to lay back. Her turn to let him enjoy the taste and feel of her. To make her shatter. But he couldn't bring himself to wake her, not just yet.

Instead, he brushed his lips over her shoulder, then sat up, noticing for the first time the scent of coffee drifting in from the kitchen. The smell filled the room, and he smiled with the memory of waking up to coffee every morning in the house they shared in Hades. Linda used to set up the coffee maker each night with a timer, so that it was brewed and ready before the alarm went off. Most days, she'd wake before him, then welcome him to the day with a kiss and a steaming mug.

Today, he could do the same.

He pulled on pajama bottoms and the flannel robe that still hung on a hook in what was his childhood closet. Then he padded quietly to the door, the wooden floor cool beneath his bare feet.

He opened the door slowly, trying to keep it from creaking, then he closed it behind him before heading to the kitchen. Sure enough, his mother had already brewed a fresh pot, and there were cinnamon rolls on the kitchen table. He glanced around the house for his parents, but saw neither of them. They tended to go walking in the mornings and were probably at the square right now.

He poured himself a mug, then started to pour another for Linda when he glanced out the window and saw his father standing with a woman by the fence. Not his mother. *Emma.*

Fear gripped the back of his neck. If she was here, something must be wrong.

With his mug still in his hand, he hurried into the backyard, passing his father. "Oh, good. I was just about to wake you. Emily's here."

"I see that," Winston said, tightly. "Did she say why?"

"On vacation. Doing some hiking. Said you'd texted her that you were in visiting us and that you'd love it if your paths crossed. So she figured she'd stop by. I invited her to spend the day. Figured Linda would want to see her, too. You all knew each other in Hades, right?"

"Yes, sir, we did." His parents hadn't been tuned in to the real details of his life in Hades, but they'd seen the fake veneer he'd spread over his life and work. Emma—or rather, Emily—had been a friend who worked in the mayor's office, who'd also come to the wedding.

His father continued on to the house, and Winston hurried to the fence where Emma was waiting. "What the hell are you doing here?"

"Hello? You head off to Texas for a mysterious assignment, then the next thing I know you're calling me to track rental cars with your dead wife. Who, by the way, thinks the way to greet an old friend is to assure me that she isn't holding you at gunpoint."

She paused just long enough to take a breath, then barreled on. "And then I try to call you back and your phone is shut down. I know because I tried to track you. And that name—Tommy Bartlett with his rental car? Intel says he's hooked up with Billy Hawthorne, and that can't be good. Plus, you told me not to call Seagrave, and—"

"Please, tell me you didn't."

"No, you said not to. But, that's a pretty big ask. So, seriously, you have the balls to ask me what I'm doing here? I wanted some fucking proof of life, dude."

He dragged his fingers through his hair. "I said hotdog. Why didn't you believe me?"

She cocked her head. "Under the circumstances, would you have believed me?"

"Probably not," he admitted.

"There you go."

"Why here?"

"You're in Texas. Your parents are in Texas. It was the best starting point I could think of. Plus, I called your mom and asked last night. I told her not to say anything. That I was in the area and wanted to surprise you."

He sighed and shook his head. "Well, okay, then. I guess I should say thanks for caring."

She laughed, then leaned forward and kissed him on the cheek. "You're welcome."

"Careful, there. What will Antonio think?"

"He'll think that I was afraid I'd find you dead, and that I'm delirious with relief. Besides, you forget that we got together on a sex island. There was a threesome," she added, lowering her voice and adding a sultry tone.

"You realize I can't un-hear that."

She laughed. "I think Antonio's fine with a kiss on the cheek. We're very open-minded." She waggled her eyebrows, and he had to bite back a laugh.

"All right. You win. I am glad you came."

"Good. Now tell me what's going on."

"According to Seagrave, this is a highly confidential assignment. Honestly, that's part of the reason I'm telling you."

She took a step back, then leaned against the fence. "That's cryptic."

"And confidential. You know. I know. Linda knows."

"Understood."

"Not even Antonio."

"I get it. Now talk."

So he did. And when he was finished, she just stood for a moment, gaping at him. "Whoa."

"I know."

"What can I do?"

"Nothing at the moment. We're just waiting for Noah. This seemed like the best place to hide out."

"And the rest of it?"

He bent down and plucked a weed, then twirled it between his thumb and forefinger. "The rest?"

"You're with your resurrected wife. Are you two back together? Or are your parents going to be sorely disappointed?"

He drew in a breath, then let it out. "That's complicated."

"Always is. Tell me."

"We should go back in."

"Chickenshit. Tell me."

He glared at her, and she glared right back. Honestly, sometimes it was hell having friends who knew you.

"Fine," she said, as he stayed silent. "I'll start. Is there still chemistry?"

"Oh, yes," he said, without a moment's hesitation.

"On both sides?"

"Definitely."

"But—"

"But she's hesitant because we were both living a lie."

"And you?"

He shrugged. He'd told Linda he wanted a fresh start, and that was true. But at the same time...

Emma tilted her head, her eyes narrowed. "So how come you didn't tell me to turn around and go. That I'd butted in on a confidential mission and I should know better. You think Seagrave may be dirty, right? I might, too."

"I made a judgment call. I trust you."

"But you don't trust Linda."

He winced, realizing that was the first time that lingering fear had been fully formed. She feared their connection wasn't real, because everything had been based on a lie. But that wasn't what worried Winston. He knew damn well that what he felt for her was bone-deep, and he believed with all his heart it had been for her, too.

And yet...

"She faked her death," he said. "She walked away. And she never came back."

"I've got news for you, sport. If I thought it would save Tony, I'd do the same damn thing. It would kill me—it would suck every bit of joy right out of my life—but I'd do it in a heartbeat. And you know what else? You'd do it for her if you had to."

He stood there, battered by the brutal truth in her words.

Her smile was just a little sad. "You didn't make a mistake trusting me today. And I don't think you're making a mistake with her, either."

"Thank you," he said, pulling her into a hug, then kissing her forehead.

"Now you're just getting fresh," she teased.

"Tell Tony he's a lucky man. And Emma? Thank you for coming."

Linda was pulling on a pair of Winston's old sweatpants when he entered the room. That fashion statement was matched by a University of Texas tee. "Nice outfit," he said, grinning as he handed her a cup of coffee. "I'd planned to enjoy watching the caffeine bring you back to life, but this is good, too. You in my clothes, I mean."

He'd expected her to laugh. Instead, she only glanced at him sideways for a second, then looked down as if tying the sweatpants cord was the most difficult task she'd ever undertaken.

"Your mother is washing my things." Her words came out crisp and clipped.

"All right," he said, taking a tentative step closer. "I'll bite. What's wrong?"

Her head snapped up, her eyes flashing with heat. "We're hiding out, and you decide to have a chat with an old girlfriend?" She underscored *chat* with air quotes.

He took an involuntary step back, at first surprised by the vitriol in her voice, then amused. And then, damn him, he actually felt smug. He fought to hide the smile of victory and the swelling in his chest. "You're jealous."

Her brow furrowed and even though she was a full three inches shorter than him, she managed to look down her nose. "Fuck you."

"All right." He reached out, grabbing her wrist before she could back away and pulling her to him.

"Don't you even think about it."

"But I am thinking about it," he said, his voice low and raw. "About how much I want to undo that tie and watch those sweats pool around your ankle. How much I want to yank off that shirt and then toss you on the bed. I'm thinking about how I want to lick your nipples and then kiss my way all the way down until you're so wet that you beg me to be inside you."

He watched her face. The heat building in her eyes. The way the pulse in her neck had quickened and her parted lips that were just ripe for kissing.

"I'm thinking about all that and more."

"You're thinking about her." The words were soft and accusatory. And more of an admission than he would ever have expected from her.

"No," he said gently. "I'm not."

"Who is she?"

"Oh, sugar, you saw me talking to Emma. Emily."

Her chin lifted, and her eyes darted to the side. "You kissed her."

"I suppose I did."

Her lips pressed together, and she pulled free, then wiped her palms on the fleece of the pants. "Why is she here?"

He lifted a shoulder. "Worried when we went off the grid, so decided to do her own investigation. I told her to cool it before she fucked something up."

She nodded slowly. "You two knew each other before Hades."

"A bit," he said. "We got closer in Texas."

She didn't quite meet his eyes when she asked, "Did you sleep together?"

"What?" He took a step back, realizing in the moment that he should have seen that coming. "Oh, darlin', no. Never even came close."

She crossed her arms and cocked her head. "Really? So there was nothing between you two then or now?"

"Nothing," he said. "She's a friend. A former partner. And we work together. I love her, but like a sister." He tilted her chin up. "Okay?"

For a moment, he thought he saw relief in her eyes. Then she dipped her head and moved away from his touch. "Okay," she said with a shrug. "It doesn't matter anyway. It's not like I have a right to get jealous."

"The hell you don't." He moved closer, his hands to her shoulders. "You're my wife, remember?"

"Winston, come on—"

"*No.* You say our marriage was built on a lie, but you're only half right. The foundation was fake, but the emotion was real."

"It doesn't work that way," she protested. "The truth is kind of a big deal."

"Dammit, Linda." Christ, the woman was infuriating. They'd had something wonderful, and the remnants of that still popped and fizzled between them. "Why are you fighting this so hard? I know what I feel. And, honestly, I know what you feel, too."

"Do you? Because what I mostly feel is guilt." He could hear the anger in her voice, and the pain. "I hurt you, and I'm standing here just waiting for the other shoe to drop."

"What are you talking about?"

"Do you think I could stand to be back with you and then lose you all over again? I've had the pain once, and that was plenty."

"Why would you lose me?"

"Come on, Winston. You look at me like you're in love. You went off the rails in the hotel not because I was an operative assigned to take out a man. Your fury was at me, not the job. Because someone you love betrayed you."

She was right. And that betrayal was at the core of that lingering fear he'd just confessed to Emma. But Emma had been right—he would have left to protect her, too. Her leaving hadn't been a betrayal. It had been the ultimate sacrifice for love.

Which begged the question—if she'd loved him that deeply then, why was she so scared now?

He drew in a breath. "Linda, please," but she only shook her head.

"You never loved me, Winston. It's not calculus. It's a simple, basic truth."

"The hell I didn't," he snapped. "And don't try to say that you didn't love me."

"How could you have? You didn't even know the Linda back then."

She held up a hand to cut off his protest, and he closed his mouth, his jaw aching with the need to argue.

"You didn't," she stressed. "Not really. And someday, you'll realize that. Maybe it won't be right away, but you will, and then everything will be pulled out from under us again."

A single tear rolled down her cheek, and she slapped at it, as if angry at her own traitorous emotions.

"You're wrong," he said. "I loved *you*. Not a shadow." He reached out to cup her cheek. "I still do."

She shook her head, her expression sad. "That's not love. It's sentimentality and regret. You don't know me, Winston. You never did. You knew a woman pretending to be a bad guy pretending to be a good guy. Hell, *I* didn't even know myself."

"Linda—"

"You know it's true. And I didn't know you, either. Sleepy small town sheriff? That was bullshit."

He wanted to protest that she was wrong, but she wasn't. Every fact was exactly true. It was just the conclusions she drew that didn't match his reality.

"We're not—"

She cut him off with a raised hand. "No. Wait. Let me finish. We've been given this amazing gift to reconcile. To heal the wounds I inflicted on you. That's an incredible thing. And—and I think that maybe it's enough."

"It's not," he said.

She let her shoulders rise and fall. "Well, it's going to have to be." She drew a breath, then stood up straighter, looking suddenly businesslike. "But we're together until this Collins-Seagrave thing plays out. And we both know the attraction is real. Whatever you want, Winston. Whatever. However."

A chill cut through him and for a moment he simply stood there, studying her, his mind whirling. Then he took a step closer, letting his gaze roam over her. "Anything I want. Any desire. Any demand. Whatever I ask, you'll agree to?"

She nodded, and he noticed the way her nipples had tightened visibly beneath the thread-bare tee. "Yes," she said, then licked her lips. "The chemistry is real—I don't doubt that at all. And—well, I think I owe you this. No strings, Winston. But also no plans about a future we both know can't happen."

He drew in a breath, then moved closer. He put his hands on her waist, then slid them up beneath the shirt, feeling the weight of her breasts before he

pinched her nipples between his thumbs and fore-
fingers.

She gasped, the sound a mixture of surprise
and pleasure. Her eyes closed, and her head tilted
back. And when he slid one hand down her belly
then beneath the waistband, and then lower still
until he was cupping her sex, she was biting her lip.

"Anything?" he whispered. "Anything at all?"

"Yes. Oh, please, yes."

He withdrew his hand, releasing her nipple at
the same time.

Her eyes fluttered open.

"I appreciate the offer, darlin'," he said. "But
you don't owe me a thing."

CHAPTER TWENTY-TWO

I'm in a pissy mood when I leave the bedroom, and it only gets worse when I see Emily—I mean, Emma—laughing with Miriam and Dale in the kitchen.

She turns to me, her face alight with pleasure, and I watch the smile die as she sees my face. She covers well, though, I'll give her that. "Hey!" she says. "I was just about to tell Dale and Miriam that you and I should walk to the bakery. Bring back kolaches for breakfast."

"Great idea." I flash them a bright smile before Emma and I head for the door.

"So, this isn't turning out to be the warm and fuzzy reunion of old friends I'd hoped for," she says after we're most of the way down the block. "Is it because I seduced your husband in the backyard?"

I stop cold, look at her face, and then burst out

laughing, all the tension easing out of me as my shoulders sag with apology. "I'm sorry," I say. "I—we—I just had a thing with Winston."

Her brows rise. "A thing," she repeats, her tone lascivious. "That's probably TMI."

"Actually, no." I draw in a breath and try to get my head on straight. "I did miss you. Truly. Has Winston told you what happened? Why I'm not dead, I mean?"

She nods. The Kelloggs live only a block from the square, and we've reached the intersection. Emma points to the bakery in the next block. "Coffee and talk now," she says. "Kolaches to go."

I agree, and when we arrive, I take a seat at one of the small sidewalk tables while she goes in to get the coffee. She returns almost immediately, her expression surprised. "I've lived in cities too long," she says. "The coffee's free with purchase, and they took my word I'd be back for the actual purchasing."

"It's nice like that here," I say. "I always liked Hades, too, even with the shit storm brewing."

"Well, you had Winston."

I sigh, wondering how badly I screwed up earlier. "I did. Or at least the illusion of Winston."

"Wanna talk about it?"

"No," I say, then immediately add, "He kissed you earlier."

"Yeah. One of those pecks on the forehead that

hide wild, passionate abandon."

I almost spit the coffee I've just sipped. "I'd forgotten how much I like you."

Her smile widens. "Mutual. And maybe I kissed him to get a rise out of you. I'm brassy as hell, after all."

I sit up, surprised. "Did you?"

"No. Honestly, I didn't even think about the fact that you might be watching. But I talked with Winston. Would've served you right to try and make you a little jealous."

"Excuse me?"

"Oh, come on, Lin. I saw you two together in Hades, remember? And I saw the way he talked about you this morning. And I can see the jealousy on your face right now."

I sit back. "So?"

"You love him. He loves you. Why is the math so difficult?"

"It's not love," I say. "It's attraction."

"Maybe. Maybe not. But back then it was love."

"It wasn't. It was only the illusion of love. We were living a lie."

"Not a lie. An inconvenient foundation."

"No, that's not—"

"Just listen," she interrupts. "I've lived a lot of roles. I think you have, too. But somewhere in all of them, it's still you, right?"

I want to argue, but I can't. "Yeah. But that

doesn't mean—"

"Will you let me finish? It's like you go see a movie. And you end up bawling at the end. I don't know. *An Affair to Remember*. Or that press conference scene in *Notting Hill*. You're all beat up inside, right?"

"My life isn't a movie."

"I'm not saying it is. I'm saying that those emotions you felt are real, right?"

"It's not the same," I protest.

"Maybe not, but I'm still right."

I lean back, my brows rising.

She shrugs. "I'm a pretty confident person," she says, and I can't help but laugh.

"Yeah, I guess you are."

"Honestly, if we'd had this conversation a few months ago, I might be more Team Linda than Team Winston."

"So what changed?"

"I met a guy. We had to go undercover. Pretend like we had a relationship. Turns out he's the love of my life."

I realize I'm smiling. "That's wonderful."

"Yeah," she says. "It really is." She reaches across the table and brushes my hand. "Trust me," she says. "Quit fighting it. And quit thinking about the past. Hades is over, but Winston's still here, and I promise you he's one of the good ones. Don't fuck it up, okay?"

I nod, moved by her words.

But I can't make a promise that I don't know I can keep.

———————

There's a car in the driveway when we return, and I meet Emma's eyes, both of us wondering who it could be.

"You go ahead and take those kolaches into the kitchen," Miriam says, meeting us on the porch. "An old work friend of Winston's dropped by. Noah, he said his name was. So we told Winston we'd get out of the way. He said if we saw you on the square, that we should tell you to come join them." She smiles broadly. "So I guess I'm telling you now."

I glance toward the kitchen. "Sorry to kick you out of your house. We don't—"

Dale cuts me off with a wave of his hand. "Nonsense. It's an excuse to go out for breakfast, and that's always a treat. Go on, now. I'm sure they'll enjoy the pastries."

Minutes later, that prediction proves true, as the men pretty much attack the bag the moment we sit down.

"Do you want me to go?" Emma asks me.

I shake my head as I look at Winston. "Nope," I say, and see the smile behind his eyes.

He turns to Noah. "How about you? You okay with Emma staying?"

"Kick out Tony's girlfriend? He'd have my head."

Emma's grin lights up her face. "I recognized you right off the bat. Tony has a photo of all the Deliverance guys on his dresser," she adds, referring to the former vigilante group that Winston told me Noah had been a part of before signing on to work with Damien Stark. "But how did you recognize me?"

"Are you kidding? He talks about you so much I asked for a picture. I'm supposed to officially meet you when I'm in LA next month. Glad we got to make it happen sooner."

"This is all very cozy," I tease.

Winston's eyes meet mine. "Yeah," he says. "It is."

I tilt my head, knowing I should still be pissed about shutting us down in the bedroom this morning. And I'll get back to that eventually. Right now, though, this is about our mission.

I turn to Noah. "You're here. That means you have something?"

Noah opens his briefcase and pulls out what appears to be a latex finger. "It's a little more sophisticated than it looks."

"I hope so, because it looks like something you would buy in a Halloween store to put on the front porch and make people think that you've got dismembered fingers lying around."

"I'll see about setting that up as a side business," Noah says. "It's actually a new type of substance. And it holds a specific temperature, so we can set it at 98.6."

"Do we think that the laptop is temperature sensitive?" Winston asks.

"I don't know. But I've got the prints set up, I've got the temperature set up, and I've got a tiny electrical circuit inside the finger to simulate a pulse. You said it was important. I don't want to take any chances with whatever it is you're trying to recover."

"I appreciate it," I say. "I don't have any way to assess the viability of my information, but I was told that any wrong move and this information will self-destruct. And we really need to know what's on that laptop."

"Do you want me to try and unlock the machine myself?"

I glance at Winston. I don't want anything to go wrong, but I also worry about someone other than the two of us seeing what might be on that screen. As I anticipate, Winston seems to read my mind.

He shakes his head. "Thanks anyway, buddy. I think you've done enough. If it fucks up now, there's not anything you could do to stop it, is there?"

"No," Noah says, "there isn't. So I may as well leave you two to curse me in absentia." He pushes his chair back away from the table and Emma does the same

"Are you heading into Austin?" she asks. "I hired a car from the airport, so I could use a lift."

I glance between them and then over to Winston. "I didn't mean to run you guys off so quickly," I say.

"Of course you did," Noah says. "You need to get on with this."

I shrug. "Guilty as charged. Go away."

They both laugh, and Winston and I walk them to Noah's car. I give Emma a hug, then Noah. "Thank you for doing this and for not asking questions. Any more than you needed to anyway."

He tightens the hug and bends in close to my ear. "I don't know what's going on between you two, but I do know that man is head over heels for you. I know because I see on his face the same thing I see in the mirror when I'm thinking about my wife."

I step away, my eyes down. Not sure if I should be annoyed or insulted or what. The truth is, Noah's words make me happy. I raise my head, give him a small smile and a shrug.

Winston shakes hands with Noah, then kisses Emma's cheek.

We watch as they back out of the drive, then

turn to go back inside. As we do, Winston reaches for my hand, then stops, lowering it slowly. "Are you still pissed?" he asks.

I shake my head. "No, you were right to back away. We need—at least, *I* need—time to figure it out. Us, I mean. And I don't think either one of us has the bandwidth while we're in the midst of all this."

It's probably a cop-out, but I'm not ready to think about what Emma or Winston have said to me about the past meshing with the present. About emotional truths and literal lies.

I want him—that's undeniable—but beyond that, I'm still stumbling with our reality.

"So you're saying no," he clarifies. "But you're not saying it forever."

"I'm saying no for now," I confirm. "And I guess we'll go from there." I flash a saucy grin to lighten the moment. "Unless you just want the sex part now. I can live with that."

"I'm ignoring that," he says, but he's grinning when he extends his hand. "No, for now. It's a deal."

Relief floods my body as I take it, accepting an unspoken truce as we go back inside.

The laptop is still in my tote bag where it's lived ever since we left the Stark Century Hotel. Now, I take it out and put it on the bed in our room. I don't want to go back to the kitchen table in case

Winston's parents come home. "It just occurred to me that we don't have a charger for this thing. What if the battery's dead?"

Winston shakes his head. "There's no charging portal. The thing runs on regular double A's. Believe me, my mother has plenty of those lying around the house."

I laugh. "I guess I'm not surprised. He didn't want anything electronic coming into that machine. Any possible way to hack it, and he closed it off. Can you hack something through the electrical line?"

Winston shrugs. "Above my pay grade," he says.

"Enough stalling. You ready?"

I nod, then open the laptop and press the power button. The screen lights up and, as we'd expected, there's a message demanding that finger-print access be obtained within the next sixty seconds or else the machine is going to shut down. Three attempts to start without fingerprint access and the information on the hard drive will be erased.

"Here goes nothing." Winston takes the plastic finger and gingerly presses it onto the keypad. I reach over and squeeze his leg as he sits on the bed beside me. We both hold our breath and then there's a click and a whir and for a moment I think the screen is going to fade into grizzled static. But then, as if by magic, suddenly we see a single folder icon. It's labeled *Hawthorne*.

"I can't believe it worked." I realize I'm whispering. I take a breath. "Click it."

"Are you sure?"

"We've come this far."

He nods, then uses the trackpad to click on the folder. It opens and we both gape at it. "What the hell?" Winston says.

I stare at the screen, my thoughts echoing his question.

It's a text file with only two lines of text:

Bigelow-247
11-11-11

"What does that mean?" Winston asks.

I take his hand and twine my fingers with his. "I have no idea."

Even as I say it, there's something familiar about the message, though I can't figure out what.

I stare at it for a moment, then tell Winston that I feel like I should know what this means.

"Why?"

"I don't know," I admit. "But there's something." I exhale with frustration. "Maybe I'm thinking about the 247. That's familiar, right? Stores are open twenty-four/seven. What else?"

"Gas stations," he says. "Some restaurants,

hotels, airports, ATM machines. The list is pretty long. It could be—"

"No. No, that's it," I say, feeling as though I should actually shout *Eureka!*

"ATMs?"

"The Bigelow Hotel." I turn to him eagerly. "That's where Billy Hawthorne stays when he goes to Los Angeles. The Bigelow Hotel on Sunset."

"So 247 is what?" he asks.

"I don't know, a room?" I frown. "Except that's not safe. All those people coming and going."

"A vault," Winston says. "That's got to be it."

"A vault?"

He nods. "I've used them before on various assignments. They're easier to gain access to than a bank safe deposit box, and those hotels have long-term services. He has something stored in vault 247. I'd bet money on it."

"You may be betting our lives," I say. "If we're wrong..."

"We don't have another option. And if we check it out and fail, neither Hawthorne nor Bartlett will know, much less Seagrave or Collins."

"You're right," I say with a frown. "We're not in danger if we're wrong, but we're going to attract a lot of attention if we're right."

"Unbreakable laptop," he says with more confidence than I feel. "They won't even see us coming."

"So the series of ones is probably the passcode

for the vault," I say, and Winston nods.

"You know what this means?" I continue.

"We're going to Los Angeles?"

"Not just LA," I tell him. "We're going to the hottest party of the year."

He shakes his head, obviously confused.

"The Bigelow Hotel hosts a huge annual party. The whole hotel is taken over by people who want to see and be seen. Bartlett has gone for the last two years."

"And you know this because…"

"I read his file before Hawthorne sent me after him. He does accounting work for celebrities, the filthy rich, that kind of thing. From what I hear, it's a huge crush. Very wild. Alcohol, drugs, anything goes. No one would pay attention to us at all if we try to slip back to the vaults."

"Excellent."

"Except we have two problems. One, the party is tonight, which means we're in the wrong damn state. And two, it's ridiculously exclusive. I don't know how we can possibly get in on such short notice."

Winston frowns, his brow furrowing as he clearly tries to figure out a solution to that little problem. Then, as if he swallowed a ball of sunshine, his face lights up with his smile. "Sugar," he says, "I think I know how we can make this happen."

CHAPTER TWENTY-THREE

Ryan Hunter opened his front door and raised his brows as Winston thrust the white box at him. "I come bearing gifts," Winston said.

"I take it this is a bribe?"

Winston shrugged. "You could call it that. I need a favor. I just came back from Texas bearing my mother's cupcakes. Linda helped make some," he added, watching his boss's face for a reaction. It didn't take long. Ryan's blue eyes widened, and for a moment he was speechless. As far as Winston was concerned, that was a first.

Ryan stepped back holding the door open for Winston to enter. "What's going on?"

"Can we talk here? Confidentially I mean?" Ryan held up a finger, and gestured for Winston to follow him to the kitchen.

Ryan's wife, Jamie Archer Hunter was standing by a coffee maker, apparently waiting for it to finish brewing. She looked up, her camera-friendly smile bright. "Winston. I thought you were out of town."

"I am. Back for awhile, but not yet back at the office. I have a favor to ask your husband."

"I think that's my cue to leave."

"Sorry, kitten," Ryan said, as he casually brushed her fingertips in a way that sent melancholy rushing through Winston. He'd had that easy familiarity with Linda once. He wanted it again.

"No problem," Jamie said. "I just need a to-go cup, then I have to get to the set. A night shoot."

From what Winston knew, Jamie worked as an on-air reporter, but more recently she'd taken on some acting jobs. She was talented enough—and pretty enough—that he assumed she'd end up a huge success.

She put a lid on her coffee, then flashed that smile again at Winston. "I hope whatever you need, Ryan can take care of for you." She drew her husband close and gave him a quick kiss on the lips. "I'll see you when I get back," she said, then left them alone.

"I'm sorry to bother you at home in the evening, but I need a favor and it's urgent."

"Mission related?" Ryan asked. "Isn't the SOC running this show?"

"Yes, but this isn't something I can bring Seagrave in on."

Ryan's brows rose, and he gestured for Winston to take a seat at the kitchen table. "Well, you have my attention."

Winston cleared his throat, not wanting to suggest that Seagrave might be dirty. He didn't want to taint Ryan's impression of the man until he was absolutely certain. "Let's just say I'm cutting some corners on this assignment, and I'd rather he not know."

"All right, we'll say that. Later on you can tell me the real truth. Deal?"

Winston had to fight a smile. "Deal."

Ryan leaned back in his chair, his legs stretched out. "I don't mean it, you know. I trust you. If you need something, I'll help you get it. No strings attached."

"I appreciate that. But I'll tell you eventually. If everything turns out okay, I'll tell you simply because I'll want to give you the whole story. If everything doesn't turn out okay, you'll hear about it anyway, and not just from me."

Ryan nodded slowly. "Okay then. What exactly do you need?"

"Leah mentioned that you added some Hollywood guy to the team? Is that true?"

"Renly Cooper. Not sure how he'll take being called a Hollywood guy. He's a former Navy Seal.

Does consulting now, especially on action movies."

"I remember she said that." The idea had been so intriguing to Winston that he'd used that as his own cover with Linda when he'd caught her in the hotel room. Had that only been a few days ago? It seemed like a lifetime. "What I'm really interested in are the people he knows. Leah mentioned he'd dated some A-listers."

"Celebrity watching? I never would have pegged you for that."

"Funny," Winston said dryly. "No, I need access to a party. Apparently it's infested by celebrities, very closed, and invitation only." He frowned. "Actually, I probably could have asked Jamie. Or Damien."

"Damien and Nikki are out of town until late tonight, and while Jamie could probably pull strings, she's still climbing the Hollywood ladder. Renly's a better choice. And this way he'll feel like he's already part of the team. Will you need him on site with you? I presume this is about more than expanding your social circle."

"Honestly? I'm going to break into a vault."

Ryan burst out laughing. "Well, now I really want to hear this story once you can tell me. I can't make any promises, but I can put you in touch with Renly. Are you prepared to tell him what you're planning to do? I don't think he's going to want his

ass hanging out there without knowing what's at
stake."

It was a good point, and one that Winston
honestly hadn't considered. "I'll tell him as much as
I can, and I'll let him know the risks."

"In that case, I'll set up an introduction. When
is this party?"

"It starts at ten."

Ryan's eyes widened. "Tonight."

Winston shrugged. "I'm not one to
procrastinate."

Ryan exhaled, then stood. "In that case, I'll set
up a meeting right now."

Renly Cooper pressed the limo's intercom and
asked the driver to circle the block one more time.

"Nice transport," Winston said.

Renly grinned, his golden eyes dancing with
humor in the limo's low light. "It's not my usual
ride."

He was sitting across from Winston and Linda,
and the overhead light gleamed on the copper hair
that he no longer wore military-short. He had the
build of a Navy SEAL, that was for sure. But the
looks of a movie star. Winston wondered if that was
his ambition. And, if so, why the hell he signed up
with Stark Security.

As it stood, he liked the guy, but wasn't quite sure what to think of him. Still, he was getting them into the party, no questions asked, and Winston definitely couldn't complain about that.

"I picture you in a Porsche," Linda said, making Renly laugh.

"I get that a lot. Actually, I've got a bike, not a car. A Ducati. But I didn't think that dress of yours would ride well." He flashed a slow smile. "Not on a bike, anyway."

Linda laughed, and Winston stifled the urge to shoot Renly a harsh glare, not to mention a punch in the lip. He knew Renly was just kidding around, but Linda was his, dammit. And as for that dress, with the slit all the way up to her hip and the bodice that looked like it would fall off her shoulders in a light breeze, well ... he was already regretting the hands-off arrangement he'd set between the two of them.

Not that any of that mattered now. They were here to do a job. And one more time around the block, and it would be time to go into the Bigelow and take a giant step forward in this operation.

"—perk of the job," Renly was saying, and Winston realized he'd tuned out the conversation.

"Pardon?"

"I was telling Linda that the limo is a favor from a producer I was working with. A ragtag team of military castoffs fights a giant squid alien. And I've seen the first cut. It's surprisingly good."

Winston laughed. "And you consulted because of your vast experience with aliens?"

Renly grinned. "Well, I could tell you, but then I'd have to kill you."

"Fair enough," Winston managed to keep a straight face. And decided that he liked this guy.

"I was also saying that you need to show up to a party like this in style. Believe me, I've been dragged to several of these things."

Linda leaned forward. "You said the staff usually stays until about midnight, then the host urges them to leave?"

"The staff will be offered incentives to go home or look the other way. Since you need into the back offices, that'll be the time to do it. You won't be the only ones, though. Not everyone wants privacy at a party like this, but some prefer to at least have their own dark corner."

"Like this?" she repeated, then looked at Winston. "Like what?"

He held up his hands. "First I'm hearing of it."

"Yeah, it's one of those kinds of parties. I assume you two are at least good friends."

Linda eyed him, and if he wasn't mistaken, she looked a little smug. So much for his plan to shut it all down. "Yeah," she said slowly. "We're friends."

"Good to hear. Okay, we're almost there. I'll go

in with you if I need to, but I got you on a list. So I'm not staying unless you need me for your operation."

"Thanks, but we've got it under control."

Renly nodded as Linda asked, "Why not stay? A Hollywood party, and you're in the industry."

He shook his head. "No."

Winston waited for him to elaborate, but Renly stayed silent. "Well," he said as the valet came to open the limo's door. "We're here."

As the uniformed man helped Linda out of the limo, Renly lowered his voice. "The alarm is disabled during these parties, but it turns back on at four. And there's a guard who patrols the back area. Mostly the offices past the vault, so he shouldn't be in your way. But he does do a sweep or two in that back hallway. Avoid him. I don't have his schedule. I just know his shift ends at six."

"We'll be fine."

Renly nodded. "Remember, get to the back room when the staff leaves. You'll exit out the far side and follow the hall to the vault room. Don't shut the vault door. My source didn't know if it has countermeasures if accessed after hours. You might get stuck inside."

"But the entry code?" Winston asked. "Does it trip a silent alarm?"

"Ninety percent sure it doesn't, but you're going to have to live with that ten percent."

He wasn't happy about it, but he nodded. "How'd you get the code anyway?"

Renly shrugged. "I have my ways. And I've learned that even though I have no actual power in this industry, I am clothed with the illusion of power. I figure it'll come in handy working for the SSA. I figured I'd give it a test run."

"There's a woman working in there who spilled a few secrets, isn't there?"

Renly only grinned. "Good luck."

"I owe you one," Winston said, then slid out of the limo to take Linda's arm.

She turned to meet his eyes, hers bright. "I've never been to a party like this. Shall we?"

He hooked his arm through hers. "Let's do it."

The limo had pulled into a private entrance in the hills behind the hotel, and not the more visible public entrance on Sunset.

Two doormen took their names—fake—then pulled open the glass double doors and ushered them into the dark boutique hotel. The dim lighting was at the perfect level to keep people from stumbling in the dark while still showing off low-cut dresses, skin, and sultry glances. Even just two steps inside, it was clear this would be like no party he'd been to before.

"See anyone familiar?"

Winston looked around, noting at least a dozen Hollywood B-listers and a few top stars as well.

"It's definitely the place to be," he said, rattling off the names.

She grinned, but said nothing.

"What?"

"I know it's partly because you were raised in your father's house, but I've always loved how wide and deep your movie IQ goes. Classics, current, even TV. All that and you're saving the world, too."

"Trying to, anyway," he said. "At least a little bit of it." He nodded toward the room in general. "That's the reception area, right?"

She followed his line of sight to the area on the far side of the atrium-style room in which they were standing. "Looks like it. So we get behind the counter, then there should be an open area, right?"

He nodded, mentally following the map in his mind. "That leads to the back room, and then from there, the vault."

"And we'll see if the code Renly got for the vault room works."

"If not, we can probably hack it." His phone had some interesting SSA software. "But hopefully it won't come to that. Especially since I'm not sure how we could manage that discreetly."

"We'd have to hope that anyone nearby is otherwise engaged." She glanced around the room, then looked back to him with a seductive smile. "That certainly seems to be the case out here."

True enough. While he'd anticipated mingling

and chatting, apparently this party didn't go in for such nonsense. People were pairing up—and not just in twos. If the area had been full of cash registers, they could have emptied them and no one would even notice.

"Well, hi there."

Winston turned to the voice behind him. A pert blonde with short, curly hair was standing with a tall, broad-shouldered man with commanding eyes who looked like he would have been equally comfortable in a boardroom. Winston recognized him as Matthew Holt, one of Hollywood's power players—and a man with a dark and dangerous reputation.

Winston reached for Linda's hand as he nodded to the couple in greeting.

"We're going over there," the blonde said, indicating a dark corner on the far side of the lobby. "You're welcome to join us."

"Oh," Winston said, the word almost a stutter. *Dammit. He should have been prepared for this...*

"That's so tempting," Linda said, snuggling against his side. "But he just made me the most decadent promises, and I'm not a girl who likes to share."

"Oh, but—"

"Come on, Carrie," Holt said. "We'll find you another temptation." He looked Linda approvingly up and down, nodded at Winston, then took Carrie's elbow and led her away.

"Was she asking what I think—"

"Yes," Linda said, tugging him in the opposite direction toward the reception counter. "And you can thank me later for saving your ass. And other parts of you."

She pulled him to a stop, then pressed up against him, her arms hooked around his neck. "Or maybe you wanted to? I mean, you said no to me, but maybe that didn't include all women." She lifted herself on her toes and brushed her lips over his ear. "Or did it?"

"Stop it," he said, willing his body not to respond and failing miserably.

She made the kind of throaty noise designed to turn him on. "Well, you're interested, at least." She squirmed against him, making his cock wake even more. "I can tell that much."

"Mission," he said firmly, trying to keep his voice stern. "The staff's about to leave. Let's get to the back room."

"Yes, sir." She pulled playfully away, then took his hand.

"Wait," he said, tugging her to a stop. "Take this." He dug into his jacket pocket and pulled out the ring he'd taken from her that very first night.

"What—"

"In case we need it," he said, slipping it onto

her finger. Neither one of them was armed. Renly had told them about the metal detectors. So if the situation got bad, that ring might be their most powerful weapon.

She held up her hand, staring at it for a moment. Then she tilted her head back and met his eyes. Maybe it was the light, but there was something about her face. Open and happy, and yet her eyes glistened with the hint of tears.

"Linda? What is it?"

"I just realized I hadn't really been sure. Not since we walked out of that hotel room in Austin."

"Sure about what?"

Her bare shoulders rose and fell, making that thin dress all the more enticing. "About whether you believed me. Really trusted me." She lifted the ring. "But I guess you do."

He cupped her chin as he bent to brush a soft kiss over her lips. "I do," he said. "I didn't when I first saw you. I didn't when I tied you down. I probably shouldn't have when you held that broken glass at my neck, but I did. And now here we are, and I trust you completely. But maybe I should have actually told you that."

"You just did," she said, waving the ring. "Come on."

She led him through the crush of the crowd, past the reception counter, and on toward the celebrated back room. He pushed the door open, and they stepped into the area. Darker than the first, it was lit by candlelight. The room was some sort of lounge for the staff, and there were padded benches, couches, and chairs scattered throughout the area.

Linda tugged him to a stop just past the threshold. "The door to the hall we need is over there," she said, nodding to the corner that Renly had described. "Looks like we should have gotten here sooner."

He frowned, noticing the couple in an intimate embrace right by that door. "Well, we have time before the staff leaves. They can't stay there all night."

Linda's hand was still in his, and now she squeezed it before giving it a tug. "I have a better idea." She started to lead the way toward the door and the couple.

"What are you doing?"

"They'll either get embarrassed and leave if we go park ourselves over there, or they'll ask us to join them, in which case we can suggest someplace a little more secluded. Either way, they clear out."

It wasn't a great plan, but it *was* a plan, so he followed her lead to within about a meter of the other couple, who were half-undressed and barely even acknowledged they were there.

Linda leaned against the wall, and he bent

forward. "They aren't even remotely interested in us," he whispered.

"Good," she said. Then, before he could protest, she took his hand and pressed it to her breast. He started to pull away, but she held it firmly in place with one hand while the other cupped his ass.

"Linda, no. We had a deal."

"No, you had an ultimatum." She took her hand away long enough to reach up and pull down the strap of her gown on one side, freeing her breast.

"Christ, Linda."

She held his gaze as she loosened the other strap, so that his hand on her breast was the only thing keeping the material in place.

"Fuck your rules," she whispered. "We're here, and we have time, and I want you. I want *this*," she added. "You say we didn't know each other back then? So what? We never did anything like this in Hades, but I want it now. I want *you* now."

She was breathing hard, her expression full of fierce passion.

"So you tell me, Winston," she continued, as his heart pounded in his chest and his cock took control of his rational thoughts. "Do you want me like this? Or do you just want to walk away?"

CHAPTER TWENTY-FOUR

I expect him to push me away—gently, perhaps, but I still expect him to say no. He'd set limits, after all, and I'm most definitely crossing the line.

Which is why I gasp when he moves his hands to cage me against the wall, then roughly closes his mouth over mine. It's a brutal, claiming kiss, and the fiery passion of it shoots straight to my core. *I want this*. I want his touch. I want everything.

And I even want it here. Crazy, maybe, but I want to prove to him and the world that I belong to his man. That there is a raw, primal, unbreakable heat that crackles between us, wild and intense.

"I thought you didn't want this," I say.

"I want you." The words have a hard edge, and I want to cling to them. To hide behind them and use them as shelter. Is it really me he wants, or is it the woman from long ago? Or simply a woman to touch?

As if he reads my mind, he unties the other strap, so that now both my breasts are bare in this hallway. "You're mine," he says. "Then, now, forever. I know it. And I'm going to make it my mission to make sure you know it, too."

"I—"

He silences me with a kiss, one hand cupping a breast as the other slides down to find the slit in this skirt. "Is this really a conversation you want to have?" he murmurs, his mouth at my ear as his hand finds my tiny thong panties. He tugs them aside, his fingers sliding deep into me. "Oh, sugar, you do like this."

"Yes," I whisper. I'm desperately wet, my skin feels on fire, and my nipples are so tight it's painful. I can hardly say no.

"Tell me you're mine," he says, pinching my clit and making me gasp. We've never played rough before. Tying me up at the hotel was a first. This is another one. And, yeah, I like it.

"Say it," he demands.

"I'm yours. You know I am."

The word is barely out of my mouth when I gasp—he's ripped the tiny thong right off my body.

I barely notice as he shoves it into his pocket, then lifts my leg, hooking it on his hip. My eyes widen, as he unzips his fly. "Are you sure?" I whisper, but even as I ask, I'm reaching for his cock, then slowly stroking it as he groans into my ear. My entire body tight with need, my sex throbbing in anticipation of this naughty, wonderful game.

"When in Rome," he says, then kisses me, long and deep. "Put your arms around my neck," he orders, and I do. My leg is still on his hip, and he uses one hand to hold my ass and another to guide himself to my entrance. Anyone looking will know exactly what we're doing, but I doubt anyone is looking. There's a couple just a few feet away, and I'm not paying the slightest attention to them, after all.

"Please," I beg as the tip of his cock teases me. He moves his hands to grip my hips as his own shift, and then he kisses me hard to block my cry of pain mixed with ecstasy as he fills me in one strong, deep thrust.

He holds me one-handed as I cling to him, my back against the wall as he fucks me hard. His hand teases my clit, and I let my mind think about where we are and what we're doing. I'd lost this man years ago, and now I'm in his arms at the hottest, sexiest Hollywood party, and he is making me go completely out of my mind.

The world really is a damn funny place sometimes.

"Come for my baby," he says, his sultry words filling my head. I don't want to. I want this to last. But his cock and his hands are running the show. He's playing me like an instrument, and when he whispers, "Now," my entire body clenches and shakes, and I have to bite his shoulder to keep from screaming as the orgasm crashes through me, again and again until, finally, reality returns and Winston sets me on my feet, then pulls out a handkerchief and gently cleans me up.

He glances toward the door, where the other couple was embracing only moments before. "They're gone," he says. "But if it was a competition, I think we won."

I laugh against his shoulder as I put my dress back together, my face warm from what is now a full-body blush. "I can't believe we did that." I tilt my head up to look at him, feeling suddenly shy. "But I liked it."

Heat still lingers in his eyes, and the corner of his mouth curves up. "So did I, darlin'."

He bends, then kisses me so tenderly I want to melt into his arms. I feel like something's shifted between us, but I don't know what, and we don't have time to analyze it. "The door," I say. "We should go before someone else comes to take advantage of the dark."

He nods, and we cross the short distance to the door. The keypad is exactly as Renly had described and we punch in the code that he'd given us, hoping his source was accurate. There's a beep, then a click as the lock releases. We open it just enough to squeeze through, then shut it behind us.

"Will I jinx us if I say that was easy?"

I can barely see Winston's grin in the dark. "Don't say it. Just in case." He takes my hand. "Come on," he urges, as we hurry down the dark hall until we reach the door to the vault.

"Here's where we find out just how spectacular Renly is in bed," I say.

Winston laughs. "What the hell?"

I shrug, though he can't see me. "That woman gave up a lot giving him this code and the one into this hall. All I'm saying is that I hope whatever she got or whatever he promised was worth it."

"Guess we'll find out." He punches in the entry code that Renly had given us, each press making a sharp little ping. I'm holding his hand, and my grip tightens with ever note. I turn my body, scanning the hall for anyone who might be barreling down on us, but if anyone is in the dark, they're not showing themselves.

"We're in," he says, and we slip into the vault, propping it open with my shoe as a defense against the locking failsafe that Renly had mentioned.

"There," I say, using my phone for a light now that we're away from any potentially prying eyes. "Box two-four-seven."

He nods, the motion tight. "Try the combination. 11-11-11," he reminds me.

I do, punching in the series of ones, or trying to anyway. But nothing happens except, after I press *enter,* I hear a low buzz, like the sound a loser on a TV game show hears.

"It doesn't want six digits," I say. "Maybe those aren't ones." I try using the alphabet, except when I look at my phone, I realize there is no letter associated with the number one. Or eleven, for that matter. "*Fuck.* We have the wrong code."

"No," he says, his voice hard. Urgent. "No, I refuse to believe that. We're here at a hotel he used to frequent at a vault number he referenced. We punched in the code he wrote down for himself."

"Except there's a flaw in your logic," I point out. "Because the passcode isn't work—*oh.*"

He turns to me, the light from his phone shining on me like a spotlight. "What?"

"It was for him. Just like you said. It's not the passcode. It's a clue to the passcode."

"Great," Winston says. "Terrific. And if he were alive and standing beside us, this would be no problem at all."

"Binary," I say. "The guy was obviously a techie. Ones and zeros, right? The combination is in binary."

"What's a binary 11 converted to decimal?" he asks, and I spread out my hands.

"How the hell do I know?"

He shakes his head, proving that there is a reason both of us are in the field and not writing code.

"Hang on," he says, doing a search on his phone, which, miraculously, has service. "It's 3," he says. "Try 3-3-3."

I do.

Nothing.

"I'm right," I insist. "This is Bartlett's note to himself. Like me writing CT on my grocery list when I need coffee and tea. It's binary," I say, fiddling with the binary converter I've pulled up on my own phone. "But we're missing something."

"Maybe. But I don't know what."

Neither do I. Or maybe I'm getting close. But it doesn't matter because right now the guard Renly warned us about is making his rounds in the hallway.

Winston's heard him, too, and he kills the light on his phone. There's a small glow from the LED lights on the various boxes combination pads, and it's just enough for me to see his face pass by.

I point to the vault door and my shoe. *Should we risk it and take it out?*

The footsteps get closer.

He shakes his head, and I get it. If the door shuts, we're most likely stuck until morning, and getting out when someone accesses the vault would be an even bigger clusterfuck.

I reach for my thigh holster, only to remember I'm not wearing it. All I have is my ring, and it requires an element of up close and personal.

The steps are closer, and I see the door move slightly. Without conscious thought, I tear open the bodice of my dress, then throw myself into Winston's surprised arms.

I kiss him, my heart pounding, hoping I'm right and it's only a guard and not whoever was chasing us outside of Thrall, Texas.

"Hey! You can't—"

I turn, completely bare-breasted, and, as I'd hoped, this poor guard stumbles.

As he does, I rush forward and tap his neck with the ring. The ring has two needles. One, a powerful sedative. The other a poison. I have the ring turned to extend the sedative's needle, and as soon as the full dose empties into the soft skin at the back of his neck, the guard collapses into my arms.

"Nice," Winston says, looking at me with an expression I don't quite recognize.

"What?" I ask, as I try to fix the dress to no avail.

He passes me his jacket. I take it gratefully and am slipping it on when he says, "You, in action. It's impressive."

"You've seen me in action before."

"I did. That was impressive, too. But my assessment was colored by emotion. Today, I'm crystal clear."

I smile. "No emotions tonight?"

"No bad ones," he says. "Well, not toward you. I'll cop to frustration."

"Sixty-three," I say, then add, "Go try sixty-three. That's our number in decimal form, without the hyphens."

He tries. It fails.

"*Shit.*"

"No," Winston says. "I think you were onto something. "The hyphens. It broke the number up into three sections. Three digits."

"A three-digit combination," I say. "But—"

"Zero-six-three," he says. "That's got to be it."

I hold my breath as he punches it in, then suck in air when the box clicks and the little door opens. "Good job," I say.

"You got us there. Binary. I don't think I would have thought of it."

"You can praise my brilliance all you want later. Right now, let's see what's in there."

It's a solitary letter-sized envelope, and although I want to look now, the guard is starting to stir. Winston gives it to me to tuck into the jacket's interior pocket, and he pulls the guard away from the door as I close Bartlett's box, then go to retrieve my shoe.

The guard has a keycard hanging from an extendable cord on his belt, and we grab that, then head down the hall in the opposite direction from the party. We leave the guard locked in the vault, knowing he'll be discovered at six when the shift changes. I doubt he'll wake up until well past eight, though. Either way, in the grand scheme of things, we don't have much time before someone realizes we've been there.

There's an employee exit down the hall, and we hurry that way. The guard's card lets us out without tripping any noticeable alarm, and we both breathe a sigh of relief along with the cool, night air.

We're on the side of the building now, and I can hear the traffic on Sunset. We walk down the hill, trying to look casual until we're past the hotel's rear entrance. Then Winston uses his phone to request a ride share, and soon enough we're heading back to Ryan's house where we'd met with Renly earlier so that we can retrieve the rental car. Then we head to Winston's house in the Pacific Palisades.

"Should I open it?" I ask once we're underway. I don't bother saying that I mean the envelope. He knows.

Winston shakes his head. "No matter how this goes, it's going to be bad news for one of us. I'd like to be home with Tiny and a bottle of whiskey. And you," he adds with a smile for me.

I nod. He's right. A car's no place for news like this.

"Who's Tiny?" I ask.

"A chocolate lab. Ten years old, mostly blind, a bit lame, and as sweet as he can be."

I smile. "One of your rescues."

He nods. "I ended up at the shelter because of you."

"Winston..."

"No," he says, "I don't mean it like that. I'm saying that part was good. Tiny's been an important part of my life, and in a strange, weird way, I can thank you for that."

"Oh," I say, the word sounding small.

He turns long enough to flash a quick smile, and we drive the rest of the way in silence.

Since we'd taken the rental from the airport directly to Ryan's house, this is the first time I've seen the charming white house. It sits on a hill, and though I can't see the ocean from here, I have a feeling that the view from the inside is spectacular.

"I have you to thank for this, too," he says, as we pause on the front porch.

For a moment, I don't understand, then realization hits. "The life insurance."

"Mmm," he says in acknowledgement.

"Although now I should probably look into returning that."

I wince. "Ouch. And sorry."

He waves it off. "I used it to invest in real estate here and in Orange County. Plus, I have a solid income from Stark Security. Returning the money won't be a problem. But even if it was, I'd rather you be alive than my bank account be full."

I reach over and take his hand, too moved by his words to say anything. For a moment, it feels like time stops. Then I clear my throat. "Right, so, I guess we need to get inside and check this out."

"Yeah," he says, "We do."

As I'd imagined, the interior of his place is lovely. No clutter, minimal furniture, and a stunning view. "I wish it were day so I could see the ocean better," I admit.

"It will be tomorrow," he says, and I realize the underlying assumption. No matter what happens next, at the very least, I'm staying here for the rest of the night. I look at him, wondering where his head is. He abandoned his no gratuitous sex policy at the party, but that was almost like taking one for the team. So have we broken down that wall? Or was that incredible experience a one-off?

The question, however, isn't one that ranks right now. We have an envelope to open.

He nods to the sofa. "Coffee?"

"Please." To be honest, I'd prefer the whiskey

he mentioned earlier, but it's been a very long day, and depending on what's in this envelope, it's going to get harder for one of us.

I ignore the sofa, choosing to join him in the kitchen. It's big and roomy, and I lean against the counter and check out the house from this vantage point. "I love your place," I say, and he grins. "Where's Tiny?"

"At a sleep-over." He holds up his phone. "Leah texted that she didn't have the chance to bring him back today."

"Leah?"

"My partner," he said. "At Stark Security. She volunteered to keep him at her place while I was in Texas. He's buddies with her dachshund."

"Seriously?"

"They make a cute couple." He passes me a coffee. "You realize what we're doing, right?"

I nod. "Fine. Time to stop procrastinating." I reach into the interior pocket of his jacket and pull out the envelope. Then I meet his eyes. "Do you want to do the honors?"

"Go ahead."

I manage a quick, curt nod, then slide my finger under the flap. There are two photographs and a folded sheet of paper covered with cramped handwriting. But all I have to see is the first photo—Billy Hawthorne standing on the deck of a boat I recognize. A yacht I've been on at least a dozen times for lazy afternoons on the lake.

The yacht my boss keeps moored at a marina on Lake Erie.

And he's right there in the picture, standing alongside Billy Hawthorne, as cozy as you please. *Dustin Collins*.

The man I thought of as a father.

And now I know he's as dirty as sin.

CHAPTER TWENTY-FIVE

"I'm so sorry," Winston says, and I look up at him through tear-filled eyes, hating the weakness that keeps me from being stoic about this.

"Have you looked through the rest?" I ask.

"Another photo of Hawthorne with Collins plus Bartlett's notes. Things he was going to testify about. It's a lot. And he makes clear that he's been working with Seagrave to bring Collins down."

I hug myself. "Well, that's good for you." I draw a breath. "I should go change. You need to call Seagrave. He's going to want to deploy a team right away."

"I know," he said. "I'll take care of it." He hesitates. "I'll toss your clothes in the wash so you have them for the morning. Right now, you should get comfortable. I've got a robe on the back of the bedroom door. Or do you want me to find you some pajama bottoms and a tee?"

"The robe is fine," I say gratefully. Then I go to change, my head full of regret and betrayal and self-loathing since I never once had even a hint that the man who'd been like a father to me was also a traitor.

I tug the ring off and put it in the interior jacket pocket before laying the suit coat across the bed. Then I step out of the mangled evening gown that Ryan lent me, hoping that Jamie won't be too annoyed. I consider tossing it, but a tailor might be able to work some magic.

Then I stand naked for a moment, unsure of what to do now. *It's over.* Our part is done. By the time I go back into the living room, a Chicago-based SOC team will be prepping to raid Dustin Collin's house as well as Billy Hawthorne's.

How could I have been so wrong about Collins?

There's a tap at the door, and a soft, "Can I come in?"

"Sure. Yes. Of course." My voice is flat, belying how much I want him to hold me.

He enters, and I move to sit on the end of the bed. "I'm so sorry," he tells me again.

"I know. Me, too."

"I called Seagrave. He offered to meet us at the SSA in the morning to fill us in on how the raid went. Emma and Renly will join us, since they helped out. And, of course, Ryan will be there. Damien Stark, too, most likely."

"Really? Well, okay. That sounds great." It *should* sound great. But I still feel numb.

Winston sits on the bed next to me and takes my hand. "The pain will ease, but it won't go away."

My throat is thick when I swallow. "I know." I sigh. "I just don't know what to do. Right now, I mean."

"You're going to do what you always do. You survive. You get through it. You make your way. I didn't do that after I lost you, and I should have. Working at the SSA has been the best decision that I ever made. I like knowing that I'm making a difference."

"I do too. It's just—" I cut myself off, then close my eyes so I can gather myself. "It haunts me, you know."

"Collins? Of course, it does."

"Yes, but it's more than me believing his lie. It's that—God, Winston, don't you get it? He authorized hits that Hawthorne assigned. He'd tell me that the target was an enemy of the state, on an authorized kill list, but now—"

"Now you're wondering how many people you took out who should have stayed alive."

"If Collins really is dirty, then it's inevitable, don't you think?"

He nods and squeezes my hand, but he doesn't say anything. What could he say?

"The only comfort I have is that I haven't actually executed that many people over the years," I say. "It's mostly been relocations into witness protection. Of course, Collins could have diverted them somewhere else to take them out himself, but at least I don't know about it. Which is horrible to say, but makes my conscience rest easier."

"I get it. And your conscience should rest easy no matter what. We follow orders, and it's not your job to look at your commander and try to decide if he's dirty. That's not supposed to be something we have to face."

"But apparently it is."

"I know." He cups my face. "Baby, I'm so sorry." And then, before I even think about what I'm doing, I've moved in for a kiss. A long, deep kiss, that makes me think that so long as I'm with this man, I can get past even the guilt that I feel knowing that I may have killed innocent people.

Gently, he pushes me away, and I close my eyes, a bone-deep sadness washing over me. "Darlin', if this is what you want, I'll be with you now because you need it. But after that—"

He cuts himself off with a shake of his head. "Linda, baby, I want what we had, not a casual fuck or two to make us feel better. I told you that in Llano, and I don't regret breaking that rule last night. I'll break it now because I think you need me. But this is the last time. I think we both know it has to be. I'm a strong guy, but at the end of the day, my heart's pretty damn fragile. I want what we had," he says. "Or nothing at all."

I blink, releasing the tears that have pooled in my eyes. "We can't get back what we had," I tell him, hating the pain that I see cut across his face, even as I feel the swelling of my own heart. "I've told you before—it wasn't real."

"Lin—"

I press my fingertip over his lips. "But here's the thing—I don't care."

His eyes crinkle in confusion, but he says nothing, so I barrel on.

"I don't care if it wasn't real in the past. Don't you get it? It's real now."

He stares at me, his face completely expressionless. "What are you saying?" Unlike his face, there's emotion in his voice. An edge. As if he's just waiting for me to push him over a cliff.

I hadn't planned to say any of this, but it's all there, pouring out of me. I think I started to realize the truth in Llano, and last night—that desperate, primal need for him—sealed it. "I'm saying that the past was wonderful," I tell him. "At least until that part where I died. But that's not something we can build on."

"Linda, please don't—"

"No. Hear me out. We *can't* build on it, but I don't think it matters." I pause as I gather my thoughts. More and more I'm realizing how much I've missed him. How much he meant to me. And how much I still want him in my life.

"This isn't about what *was* between us. It's about what *is* between us. It was different before, because our conversations never touched on our real lives. The deep down truth, I mean. But I still loved you, even if it was all an illusion. But now—"

I see a hint of trepidation in his eyes and hurry to finish.

"Now I know the real man. And I've fallen in love with him all over again."

His head tilts to that side with an intensity familiar to me from those long years ago. "Baby," he says. "What exactly are you saying?"

"That I love you," I tell him. "Isn't it obvious?"

"Oh, Christ, darlin', I love you, too."

"I know," I start to say, but he cuts off the words with a kiss, his mouth claiming mine as he gently pushes me back on the bed, then tugs on the sash to open the robe. "I want you," he whispers.

"And you have me," I say.

We share a smile before he kisses me, starting at my lips and working all the way down my body. We make love slowly and sweetly, and nothing at all like last night. But it's wonderful and it's perfect.

Most of all, it feels like coming home.

CHAPTER TWENTY-SIX

Despite the horrific circumstances under which I'm meeting the team at Stark Security, I can't seem to get rid of the grin that keeps demanding to touch my lips. A decidedly sensual smile that has been threatening to light up my entire body all morning.

"You're glowing," Winston murmurs as we enter the SSA.

"If I look unprofessional, I blame you."

"I can live with that." He tugs me to a stop, hooks an arm around my waist, and then kisses me as Damien Stark walks by, as gorgeous in person as he is in the press and on social media. He's with his wife, a stunning former beauty queen who now runs some sort of tech company, and another blonde I don't recognize.

"Winston! Not in front of everyone." I'm not

sure whether to laugh or smack him. All I know is that I couldn't have survived the horror of finding out the truth about Collins without him. Honestly, I'm not sure I could stand to be without him, period.

"It's okay," he teases. "I told them we're married. Besides, hardly anyone is here."

He's right about that. I glance around the contemporary office space in The Domino, a business park in Santa Monica that was designed by Damien Stark's half-brother, Jackson Steele. Other than the Starks and Nikki's friend and the folks already gathered in the glassed-in conference room, the office is empty. Winston told me that it's Ryan's policy that unless being in the office is essential, any work that needs to happen on a weekend at the SSA is supposed to be handled virtually.

"Well, in that case." I rise up on my toes to kiss his cheek. "Enough flirting." I draw in a breath, letting myself think about why we're here. "We have a meeting."

I see the compassion when he meets my eyes. "We do."

"I'm okay," I tell him. "I was a mess last night, but you made it better."

He says nothing, but takes my hand as we go to the conference room. Emma's deep in conversation with Anderson Seagrave, who looks up at me and smiles. I return the grin, then come to both of them.

"Uncle Andy," I say, laughing as I bend to give him a hug.

"It's good to see you," he says, "despite the difficult circumstnaces."

"You, too," I say, shooting Emma a quick smile as well.

Ryan is seated and talking to Renly as I return to my side of the table and Winston.

Nikki and the blonde have disappeared. I glance around and see them at one of the computer consoles in the main office area, Nikki standing behind the other woman and pointing at something on the screen.

"Software installation."

I turn to find Damien Stark standing behind me. That's all he's doing, and yet he has a complete air of command, and when he extends his hand and smiles in greeting, I can't help but feel as though I've passed some sort of test.

"Um, installation?"

"My wife, Nikki, and the one with the curlier hair is Abby Jones, her partner."

"Did you say Abby Jones?" Renly stands up at the table, his head angled to peer around us and into the room past the glass. "Did she grow up around here?"

Damien frowns. "I think so—wait, yes. She grew up in Santa Clarita."

Renly leans back, an odd smile on his face. "Well, what do you know..."

I'm curious enough to ask what he means, but that's when Seagrave says, "I have an update."

He wheels closer to the conference table and puts down his phone. I glance at Winston, and we both take a seat.

Immediately, Seagrave turns to look at me, his gold-flecked brown eyes and graying temples that give him an air of authority. "Linda," he says. "I'm sorry about Collins, but deeply relieved that you are not what we believed."

I nod, fighting the urge to reach for Winston's hand. This is a professional debriefing. Not a wake, after all.

"Obviously, you—and the rest of you—have personal knowledge or have been briefed on the situation. Though it gives me no pleasure, I'm sorry to report that we have confirmation beyond the material in that vault that Dustin Collins was intimately involved in a number of foreign and domestic criminal operations. He's in custody now, and we expect to find more evidence in the coming days, beyond what the team already recovered from his home."

My mouth is dry, and despite my attempt at professionalism, I sag with relief when Winston reaches out to close his hand over mine.

"And Hawthorne?" I ask.

Seagrave's face hardens, the sympathy fading. "We have no sign of him. It's possible Collins was able to send him some sort of last minute signal, warning him to stay away from his home and boat."

"So he's in the wind," Ryan says.

"Our best operatives in the Chicago area are on it. We'll find him." He holds out his hands. "That's all we have at the moment. Linda, considering your knowledge of both men, I'd like you to come to the SOC tomorrow for an interview."

"Of course."

"Also, I'm sure you're aware that the SOC has watched you for some time. Granted through the wrong lens, but either way, we can't deny the extent of your skills. I know you must be feeling dislocated, and I hope it eases you somewhat to know that you have an offer to join the SOC if and when you want the position."

"Oh."

I glance at Winston, who's looking not at me, but at Ryan.

Seagrave laughs, and I think I'm the last to get with the conversation when he says, "Then again, you may have competing offers."

I look toward Ryan, then Damien. Both men smile. Beside me, Winston squeezes my hand. "Thank you. It's a lot to consider." I turn to smile at Winston. "But I will consider it."

The meeting wraps up quickly after that, and

Winston and I ask Renly and Emma if they want to come by Winston's house for a quick drink and a recap of the whole story in which they'd both played key roles.

Renly looks like he's going to decline, but then he shrugs and accepts. I turn around, then smile when I realize that Abby's gone. But I feel no guilt. I'm sure they can get reacquainted later. As for Emma, it turns out that Tony is with some friends until the evening, and she's all in.

We came in Old Blue, Winston's battered pickup truck that I both love and remember from Texas. We head back first, and Winston parks in the drive instead of the garage so that it's easier to see which house is his.

We order in, and soon the four of us are laughing over delivered quiches, fruit salad, and mimosas made from the juice and champagne in Winston's refrigerator.

"I'm impressed you have this," I tell him.

"The champagne's leftover from Christmas," he tells me. "Consider it well-aged. And as for the orange juice, I'd just gone grocery shopping before I was shipped off to Texas to reunite with my wife."

"Reunite," Emma says. "I like that. Much better than *hunt her down.*"

I scowl. "Do you want a mimosa or not?"

"Yes, please. I'll be good."

I pour, then pass it to her. "Why do I doubt

that?"

She meets Winston's eyes. "It's like she knows me..."

We all laugh, and Emma turns her attention to Renly. "So?"

His eyes widen as he looks at all of us. "I need a little bit more to go on."

"Abby," Emma says. "What's the story?"

His eyes crinkle at the corner, and I think his mouth curves into the slightest smile. "No story," he says. "She was just one of my friends in junior high."

I look at Winston to see if he's buying that, but unlike me and Emma, he doesn't seem interested.

I shrug, then lead everyone to the living room.

All in all, we spend a solid three hours laughing and talking. And while I hadn't been thinking about it consciously, I know now that I won't be joining the SOC. I like Seagrave just fine, but I want to work with these new friends. And, of course, with Winston.

"That was nice," Winston says as we stand on the driveway a half hour later. With the breeze, it's actually chilly, and since I have no coat of my own, I'm back in Winston's suit coat, which pairs well with my jeans. Tomorrow is definitely a shopping day.

Emma is long gone, having hurried away the moment Tony texted that he was home. Renly has just left, and I can still hear the roar of his Ducati in the distance.

"I'm going to run down to the corner and get some more juice," Winston says. "Come with?"

I shake my head. "Nope. I'm going to take a walk to the end of the block to check out the view. Then I'm going inside, getting undressed, and waiting for you in bed with a half-filled glass of champagne. To which you can add juice when you return."

His forehead crinkles. "Add juice," he repeats. "Is that a euphemism?"

"You have a dirty mind," I say primly as he slides into the driver's seat. "I love that about you." I bend to give him a quick kiss, then walk down the driveway to the street. I give him one last wave, then put my headphones in and turn on some music. It's been a long time since I've been able to just walk and listen, and I—

Ka-boom!

I jump, turn around, and my scream sticks in my throat. Old Blue is alight with flames. *A car bomb.*

Winston was in the car.

Oh, dear God, no. Please, please, no!

I try to run, but it's as if my legs are spaghetti, and I sink to the asphalt. A van stops behind me, and I turn around, intending to beg them for help.

Instead, I scream.

CHAPTER TWENTY-SEVEN

W inston sat in the cab of Old Blue, and watched as Linda walked down the road, looking sexy as hell in his jacket. He smiled to himself, not quite able to believe that she was truly his again. He started to pull the car door shut, thinking that he would pick up flowers along with the orange juice, then remembered that he left his damn wallet on the table by the front door.

Well, hell.

He gave the driver's side door a gentle shove with his foot, then stepped down. His eyes were still on Linda, and that was a mistake, because he lost his balance, and ended up windmilling his arms like an idiot as he stumbled forward and away from the truck, trying to right himself.

He didn't make it.

Instead, he was suddenly, strangely airborne.

He landed hard on the grass, the world having exploded around him. His body ached from the impact of his fall, and his ears rang. The smell of fuel and burning metal filled his senses.

This was more than a fall.

His mind was slow. Groggy. And nothing around him seemed to be the right color. It was all grey and, oh, man, the ringing in his ears. It was...

Explosion!

Oh, God, it really was an explosion.

Finally, in a rush, rational thought returned to him, and he shoved himself up onto his knees, looking around frantically. She was there, on the street, screaming his name as two men grabbed her by the elbows and hauled her to her feet before tossing her into the back of a black van and tearing off down the street.

No. No, goddammit, no.

He didn't remember running, but he was on the street now, the sound of sirens swirling around him. *But not for her—they were for the fire. He had to get to her. He was her only chance.*

And Old Blue was a burning husk.

Think, dammit, think.

"Get on!"

The voice was Renly's, and he gestured to the back of the Ducati. Winston didn't hesitate. He got on, grabbed hold of Renly, and prayed that this was the miracle he needed as the other man shot off after the van like a rocket.

They didn't talk—they *couldn't* talk—and it was all Winston could do to hang on for dear life as Renly swerved desperately in and out of traffic, trying not to lose the van, but also to not get too close and draw attention.

The whip of the air was bringing Winston's senses back. His skin felt raw, and he knew that he'd been somewhat singed. It could have been worse, though. He could be dead.

Linda, he realized, believed that he was.

Linda. His Linda.

It was Hawthorne. It had to be. And Winston was going to kill the bastard with his own hands, and watch the life drain out of that prick.

Finally the van pulled into the driveway of a shitty little house in—hell, he didn't even know where they were. On a street lined with shitty houses. The kind of neighborhood where everyone minded their own business and the primary employer was the street.

"We walk from here," Renly said, killing the engine as three people got out of the van. Winston recognized Hawthorne with two others.

"Get her settled for me, then make yourselves scarce," Hawthorne said. "My old friend, Linda, and I need to have a little chat."

"Any chance you're armed?" Renly said.

"Ruger LCP," Winston said. It was small, a
.380. But it was reliable and it would work in a
pinch. It had a clip, and was snug in the waistband
of his jeans, his go-to weapon when he wasn't on
the job.

"You?"

"A Glock 19," he said. "I keep it tucked into the
compartment under the seat." He opened the seat
in demonstration, revealing the small Glock 9mm
that barely fit.

"Good," Winston said. "Call for backup, then
do something about the two who are heading for
the house. Careful, they might not be alone."

"Not my first rodeo."

"Right."

"You're going for her on your own? Let me
cover you."

Winston shook his head. "For all we know
they've got monitoring equipment. If they see us
before we get Linda, we're dead, and so is she. You
want to help? Take them out. Agree?"

"Affirmative."

They waited low by the bushes as the two
thugs entered the house and Hawthorne went into
the garage. For the briefest of moments, Winston
saw her there, strapped to a chair, her tear-stained
face breaking his heart. He knew what she was
feeling—not just scared for herself, but believing
that he'd died in the explosion—and he was

damned if she was going to feel it any longer than she had to.

Slowly, he circled the house. He needed a way to infiltrate the garage without Hawthorne seeing or hearing him. But he also needed to move fast. Hawthorne was the kind to enjoy drawing out the kill, but in the end, he *would* kill.

Bottom line, Winston needed to move quickly, and he needed a clean shot. He had one chance. Miss the target, and Hawthorne would ensure that Linda was dead in a heartbeat.

One shot.

He crept around the perimeter, searching. He just needed a way in. Some way to get him a direct line of sight to Hawthorne.

A clear shot for a kill.

But there was nothing. Not on the front of the garage. Not on the western wall. Not on the back.

Then he reached the side of the garage that abutted the back yard. And there it was.

At some point, the home's resident had owned a dog. A big dog that used the garage as dog house.

It wasn't ideal, not by a long shot. But Linda needed him.

He smiled, cold and dangerous.

Yeah. He could make this work.

CHAPTER TWENTY-EIGHT

"You fucking little bitch. You goddamned whore." Billy Hawthorne paces in front of me, his white-blond hair seeming to glow in the dim light of this garage.

I just sit there, my arms and legs strapped to this wobbly old kitchen chair, as his words bounce off me as if I were a wall and they were rubber. I'm too numb to feel. *He's dead*. Oh, dear God, Winston is dead.

It feels as though the universe is punishing me, slapping me with such horrible, painful irony. Telling me that it's all over, the fight's done, and that at least I'll be with Winston again soon.

Except that's not who I am. I'm not going to submit. I'm going to fight. For myself, for Winston, and for every person Hawthorne has hurt over the years. Especially those he and Collins manipulated *me* to hurt.

So no. It's not the universe punishing me—it's Hawthorne fucking with me.

And although I don't have a clue how I'll manage it, I intend to end this guy. Or die trying, anyway.

"I trusted you, you cunt," he snarls, pacing in front of me. "I was your friend. I gave you work. I let you into my circle. And now I learn this? Let me tell you, sweet cheeks, I am very, very disappointed in you."

I want to tell him to fuck off. Instead, I keep looking straight ahead. I know Hawthorne. My reaction is what he wants. My fear is what gets him going. My hatred gets him hard.

I'm not giving him any of that.

He makes a scoffing noise, then comes closer. "Pity about your big strong man. Not so big and strong now, is he? Now he's just little bits of goo scattered all over the lawn. Serves the fucker right. Shame about that truck, I'll admit that. But the prick inside it? I got no remorse there at all."

I can't help it. I lift my eyes to look at him. But I say nothing. I still won't give him the satisfaction.

His face goes red, and he rushes forward and gets right in my face, his hands on the arm of the chair. He's so close I can smell his breath. Onions and something putrid. I want to gag.

"Say something, bitch."

I meet his eyes. I stay silent.

He pulls a knife from his back pocket, flicks open the blade. I go stiff, fear icing my blood. If I'm going to die, I'd prefer it be quick. Hawthorne, I'm sure, will make sure that it's not.

I expect to feel the steel of that blade on my skin. Instead, he starts to slowly and methodically cut my clothes off of me.

"No fast death for you," he says as he slices the seams on the jacket. "No, we're going to do this layer by layer."

He's detached the sleeves, and he slices forward, opening the armhole so he can take off the bulk of the jacket. He tosses it on the floor, and I hear a subtle clink as the ring tumbles from the pocket onto the concrete floor.

He doesn't notice, and I force myself not to look down. I continue to look straight ahead as he uses the knife to start slicing my shirt, peeling it off in strips until it's in a pile on the floor, too. I'm still in my bra with the suit's detached sleeves on my arms, and I force myself to stay still. No reaction at all.

"I'm down to skin," he says. "So do I undress the rest of you? Or do I start peeling away the skin of those lovely brea—"

He cuts himself off, and I frown, then bite back a curse when I see what's drawn his attention. *The ring.*

"Well, isn't this interesting?" He bends to pick it up. "Collins always did give his people the most interesting toys. This one has two needles, right? A sedative for most missions and a poison for those dark and dangerous circumstances."

I say nothing. He's right, of course. I'd intended to use the poison on Bartlett. It's conveniently untraceable. And later, I'd tried to maneuver it so that I could use the sedative on Winston.

That didn't go so well.

And now, because of the guard in the vault, there is only poison left in the ring.

"I'd intended to draw this out," Hawthorne says, taking a step toward me. "But now I'm thinking that a fast death might be amusing. I can watch the fear build in your eyes, as I come closer and closer, because you know exactly what's coming."

He takes another step.

"Or do you? Will you get the poison or the sedative?" he continues, obviously not realizing one needle has been emptied. "Which scares you more? Death? Or sleep and the knowledge that I can do anything to you—touch you however I want—and you'll wake up ripped apart and bleeding?"

A vile smile slithers across his mouth. "You really are such a pretty thing, and I've always wanted you in my bed. How is it you never fucked me? How is it I never made you?"

I resist the urge to spit, my mind churning for some solution. But I'm strapped down tight, and even though I could shove the chair backwards as he approaches, that would only buy me seconds.

Still, seconds are something...

"Poison or sleep?" he continues. "It's like flipping a coin. Like the lottery."

He's right there now, leaning forward, the ring outstretched. And, yeah, I claim those seconds. I lean forward, then lurch backward, trying to kick my strapped-down feet out in the process. I don't get much momentum, but I get enough, and I tilt backward at the same time that I hear a sharp *crack!*

At the same moment, something wet and sticky splatters my face and, as if in slow motion, I fall the rest of the way, landing on my back on the hard concrete, still tied to the chair.

I open my eyes, and see Billy Hawthorne fall. There's a sick crunching as he lands facedown beside me, a huge chunk missing from the back of his head.

I wrench my head around, trying to see, and manage to scoot the chair just enough to open up my field of vision.

Winston.

He's alive.

He's either alive or I'm dead and dreaming, but he has to be alive. Because there is no way in hell my subconscious would have him half in and half out of a doggie door, a Ruger tight in his hands.

"Winston?" I say. And that's when the tears start to flow.

My heart pounds as he wriggles the rest of the way in. He's at my side in an instant, using the knife that Billy dropped to cut me free. He pulls me up, then rips off his tee so that I can cover myself. He bends for a strip of my shirt, then gingerly cleans the blood from Billy off my face.

"I thought you were dead." My voice is raw from the force of my sobs.

"I almost was. I realized I forgot something. I got out of the car with only seconds to spare."

That's when I notice his clothing is singed. "They must have used a manual detonator. One of Billy's men—*oh!* There are more of them."

As I speak, the garage door rattles open. I turn, the terror fading to relief when I see Renly standing there. He gives Winston a thumbs-up, then smiles at me. "Thank God," he says. "Backup is on its way. Take your time," he adds, then walks away.

I shake my head, not certain I'm following everything.

"Those other men have been taken care of," Winston tells me. "We can stay here until the cavalry arrives. Give a statement, then go home." He cups my chin as he meets my eyes. "Sound good?"

"Better than good." Right then, covered in blood and my body aching, I've never been happier. After all, the man who'd died in front of me is standing here alive.

I swallow. "Winston, I'm sorry. I'm so, so sorry."

Confusion plays across his face. "For what, sugar?"

"For not believing that we were really in love before. I sat there in that chair certain that you were dead. I felt what you went through after I supposedly died. I made you go through that back then, and I—"

"You didn't have a choice. And we're together now."

"We were together then, too," I tell him. "And you're right. It wasn't the role we were playing, it was who we were in our hearts. I loved you then, real and true. Just like I love you now."

"Oh, baby." His pulls me close and looks deep into my eyes. "I love you, too. We're so damn lucky."

"Can I ask you something?"

"Anything," he says.

"Will you marry me again? This time in front of our friends and your family, and with our real names?"

He stokes my hair. "Funny, I was planning to ask you that very thing."

"I still have my wedding ring," I tell him. "It's in a PO Box in Chicago."

He closes his eyes, the pain on his face obvious. "I had them scour that car to find it. I finally decided whoever planted the bomb took it from you first."

I swallow the lump in my throat. "No. I went along with the fake death to protect you. But I refused to part with the ring."

"We can get a new one," he tells me, but I shake my head.

"No. That's the ring I want. It's been through a lot. So have we."

The corner of his mouth curves up. "'Til death do us part."

I can't help but laugh. "I think we'll be together a long time. We've gotten around death twice now."

"Yeah," he says, matching my grin. "We have. I love you, sugar."

"I know," I tell him, joy replacing the last remnants of this ordeal. I move closer, my arms tight around him. For a moment, I just hold him. Then I pull back a bit and look up. "Winston," I say, my voice thick. "Let's go home."

EPILOGUE

"I'm so happy you're joining Stark Security," Emma says, grinning as she takes Tony's hand. She smiles up at him. "Linda's a badass," she adds, making me laugh.

Tony's brows rise. "Coming from you, that means a lot. Seriously, Linda, it's great to have you on the team."

"I'm thrilled, too," I admit. "About all of it," I add, referring to the fact that I've not only joined the SSA's payroll, but my apartment in Chicago is now empty and the boxes of my stuff are stacked in Winston's garage. A garage that, I hope, won't stay empty for long. I've been answering ads from all over the country hoping to find a replacement for Old Blue, and I've narrowed it down. Now, I just have to keep it a secret from Winston.

As if he heard my thoughts, he looks over from

where he's talking with Renly and Nikki Stark. From what I understand, it's not common for Damien to be in on the day-to-day operations at the SSA, but this isn't a regular day. This is an after-hours celebration, complete with cocktails, to welcome me and Renly into the fold, and both he and Nikki are here, along with Ryan's wife, Jamie and a few others.

I've met everyone, I think, and I glance around the room, putting names with faces. But I don't stop to linger with my new colleagues as I head toward Winston. Right now, it's only him that I want.

For that matter, I'm ready to find Damien and Ryan, officially thank them, and get Winston home. I have plans for this evening...

He smiles as I come up, and I slide my hand into his. I'm wearing my wedding ring, though we haven't yet renewed our vows, and I feel the pressure of it as he squeezes my hand, smiling down at me with a kind of tenderness that makes me happy to be alive. More, it makes me feel like the luckiest woman on earth.

I have him again, after all. I'd lost him, and now he's back, and we're stronger together than ever. I tilt my head up to find him smiling back at me, and the love I see there makes me weak in the knees. Across from us, Renly grins. "I feel like a voyeur," he says, as a blush warms my cheeks.

I glance at Nikki, strangely self-conscious about

feeling sappy in this environment, but she's frowning at her phone.

"Sorry," she says, looking up in apology. "There's an emergency. I need to run."

"The kids?" Winston asks.

She shakes her head, her brow furrowed in concern. "No, no it's my assistant."

Across from me, Renly stiffens. "Abby? Is she okay?"

"I—I'm not sure. Sorry," she says again. "I really need to run."

"Of course," Winston says.

Renly puts a hand on her arm as she starts to pass. "Wait," he says. "I'm coming with you."

the end

I hoped you enjoyed Winston and Linda's story! And I hope you're excited to meet **Renly** in *Memories of You!*

Hollywood consultant Renly Cooper is fed up with relationships. His recent breakup with a leading lady played out across the tabloids, and the former Navy Seal is more than ready to focus on his new position as an agent at the elite Stark Security agency. He's expecting international stakes. Instead, his first assignment is to protect one of Damien Stark's friends from a stalker. A woman who, to his delight, turns out to be one of his closest childhood friends.

After a foray into online dating puts tech genius

Abby Jones in danger, she needs a bodyguard, and her business partner, Nikki Fairchild Stark, enlists help from Stark Security. When the assigned agent turns out to be her best friend from junior high—and her first crush—she's thrilled to discover he's even more delicious now. She hopes one sexy night can turn into more, but Renly is firmly in the friends-with-benefits camp.

As the threat to Abby increases, she tries to keep her growing feelings for Renly at bay. But as the sparks between them burn even hotter, can they go from friends to lovers when the first order of business is simply to keep Abby alive?

Charismatic. Dangerous. Sexy as hell.
Meet the elite team of Stark Security.

Shattered With You
Shadows Of You
(free prequel to Broken With You)
Broken With You
Ruined With You
Wrecked With You
Destroyed With You
Memories of You (novella)
Ravaged With You

And be sure to preorder *Ravaged With You*. The hero in that upcoming novel, Red, was first introduced in *Cherish Me*!

The Stark Security books are set in the world of Stark International, a world that first came to life for me in *Release Me*, Damien Stark and Nikki Fairchild's story. If you haven't read it yet, I encourage you to dive in!

Finally, be sure to keep turning page for a peek into my sexy new trilogy, My Fallen Saint!

JK

MY FALLEN SAINT
SNEAK PEEK!

"**J. Kenner knows how to deliver a tortured alpha that everyone will fall for hard. Saint is exactly the sinner I want in my bed.**"

Laurelin Paige, NYT bestselling author

The wind stings my face and the glare from the afternoon sun obscures my vision as I fly down the long stretch of Sunset Canyon Road at well over a hundred miles per hour.

My heart pounds and my palms are sweaty, but not because of my speed. On the contrary, this is what I need. The rush. The thrill. I crave it like a junkie, and it affects me like a toddler on a sugar high.

Honestly, it's taking every ounce of my willpower not to put my 1965 Shelby Cobra through her paces and kick her powerful engine up even more.

I can't, though. Not today. Not here.

Not when I'm back, and certainly not when my homecoming has roused a swarm of butterflies in my stomach. When every curve in this road brings back memories that have tears clogging my throat and my bowels rumbling with nerves.

Dammit.

I pound down the clutch, then slam my foot onto the brake, shifting into neutral as I simultaneously yank the wheel sharply to the left. The tires squeal in protest as I make a U-turn across the oncoming lane, the car's ass fishtailing before skidding to a stop in the turnout. I'm breathing hard, and honestly, I think Shelby is, too. She's more than a car to me; she's a lifelong best friend, and I don't usually fuck with her like this.

Now, though...

Well, now she's dangerously close to the cliff's edge, her entire passenger side resting parallel to a void that boasts a view of the distant coastline. Not to mention a seriously stunning glimpse of the small downtown below.

I ratchet up the emergency brake as my heart-

beat pounds in my throat. And only when I'm
certain we won't go skidding down the side of the
cliff do I kill Shelby's engine, wipe my sweaty
palms on my jeans, and let my body relax.

Well, hello to you, too, Laguna Cortez.

With a sigh, I take off my ball cap, allowing my
dark curls to bounce free around my face and graze
my shoulders.

"Get a grip, Ellie," I murmur, then suck in a
deep breath. Not so much for courage—I'm not
afraid of this town—but for fortitude. Because
Laguna Cortez beat me down before, and it's going
to take all of my strength to walk those streets
again.

One more breath, and then I step out of the car.
I walk to the edge of the turnout. There's no
barrier, and loose dirt and small stones clatter down
the hill as I balance on the very edge.

Below me, jagged rocks protrude from the
canyon walls. Further down, the harsh angles
smooth to gentle slopes with homes of all shapes
and sizes nestled among the rocks and scrubby
plants. The tiled roofs follow the tightly winding
road that leads down to the Arts District. Tucked
neatly in the valley formed by a U of hills and
canyons, the area opens onto the town's largest
beach and draws a steady stream of tourists and
locals.

As far as the public is concerned, Laguna

Cortez is one of the gems of the Pacific Coast. A laid-back town with just under sixty-thousand people and miles of sandy and rocky beaches.

Most people would give their right arm to live here.

As far as I'm concerned, it's hell.

It's the place where I lost my heart and my virginity. Not to mention everybody close to me. My parents. My uncle.

And Alex.

The boy I'd loved. The man who broke me.

Not a single one of them is here anymore. My family, all dead. And Alex, long gone.

I ran, too, desperate to escape the weight of my losses and the sting of betrayal. I swore to myself that I'd never return.

As far as I was concerned, nothing would get me back.

But now it's ten years later, and here am I again, drawn back down to hell by the ghosts of my past.

ABOUT THE AUTHOR

J. Kenner (aka Julie Kenner) is the *New York Times*, *USA Today*, *Publishers Weekly*, *Wall Street Journal* and #1 International bestselling author of over one hundred novels, novellas and short stories in a variety of genres.

JK has been praised by *Publishers Weekly* as an author with a "flair for dialogue and eccentric characterizations" and by *RT Bookclub* for having "cornered the market on sinfully attractive, dominant antiheroes and the women who swoon for them." A six-time finalist for Romance Writers of America's prestigious RITA award, JK took home the first RITA trophy awarded in the category of erotic romance in 2014 for her novel, *Claim Me* (book 2 of her Stark Saga) and another RITA trophy for *Wicked Dirty* in the same category in 2017.

In her previous career as an attorney, JK worked as a lawyer in Southern California and Texas. She currently lives in Central Texas, with her husband, two daughters, and two rather spastic cats.

Stay in touch! Text JKenner to 21000

to subscribe to JK's text alerts. Visit www.jkenner.com for more and to subscribe to her newsletter!

CPSIA information can be obtained
at www.ICGtesting.com
Printed in the USA
FSHW020508070121
77359FS

9 781949 925883